THE BIBLE RIDE

BOOK 3

THE BIBLE RIDE
BOOK 3

A Week of Passion: An Eternity of Joy

GARY W. MOON

VINE BOOKS
SERVANT PUBLICATIONS
ANN ARBOR, MICHIGAN

Vine Books is an imprint of Servant Publications especially designed to serve evangelical Christians.

Published by Servant Publications
P. O. Box 8617
Ann Arbor, Michigan 48107

Cover design and illustrations: Hile Illustration and Design, Ann Arbor, MI

99 00 01 02 03 10 9 8 7 6 5 4 3 2 1

Printed in the United States of America
ISBN 1-56955-049-2

LIBRARY OF CONGRESS CATALOGING-IN-PUBLICATION DATA

Moon, Gary W., 1956-
A week of passion, an eternity of joy / Gary W. Moon.
p. cm. — (The Bible ride : bk. 3)
ISBN 1-56955-049-2 (alk. paper)
1. Jesus Christ—Biography Devotional literature. 2. Jesus Christ—Biography—Passion Week Prayer-books and devotions—English. 3. Family Prayer-books and devotions—English. I. Title. II. Series: Moon, Gary W., 1956- Bible ride ; bk. 3.
BT306.5.M69 1999
249—dc21 99-21312
CIP

DEDICATION

I wish to say "thanks" to the Reverend John Swails—the greatest Bible scholar I've personally known—for his input. If a mistake is found in this volume, it's because I forgot to ask him about it.

I'm thankful to Mrs. Long for all her Sunday school lessons for third-graders. They were very inspirational. It's not her fault my sense of humor stopped developing at that age.

And again, I am appreciative to my daughters, Jesse and Jenna, for providing the motivation to tackle this project, and to my wife, Regina, for not complaining about the time it took.

Finally, I am appreciative to you, the reader, for investing in the cost of this ride. If enough of you go through the turnstiles, I think the Pilgrims will be off for a ride through the Old Testament.

PREFACE

A Week of Passion: An Eternity of Joy. Sounds like a romance novel, doesn't it? Well, it is. The book in your hand is about how much a hero (Jesus) loved his heroine (you). It's got fight scenes (at least one of which involves a sword), extraterrestrial appearances, a horrible murder of an innocent victim, and an ending that half the world still doesn't believe.

Oh yeah, it's also a family devotional about Jesus' last week on earth—the most important week in the history of the universe. You may have heard what follows referred to as the "Passion Narrative." But you probably never heard it like this.

If you are not already familiar with *The Bible Ride* series, you will want to read this preface. While the present volume is a "stand alone" devotion book, it is also the third installment of a three-volume series.

The Bible Ride series was born out of a desire to present all of the scenes in the life of Christ in chronological order for families to read together as part of their family devotions.

Conveniently, the Gospel writers provide us with 366 "scenes" from the life of Jesus, placed one after the other.* All of these mini-moves from Jesus' life are presented in the three-volume set. (Although some of the briefer ones have been

---

*Kurt Aland, in *Synopsis of The Four Gospels,* has compiled all of the "scenes" recorded by the Gospel writers in chronological order. They number 366. All are included in *The Bible Ride* trilogy. Some have been collapsed, however, making our total 240. Third edition of Aland's *Synopsis of The Four Gospels* published by United Bible Societies in 1972.

combined with others to make the devotions more balanced in material covered in each reading.)

The intent of *The Bible Ride* series is to take an ordinary, modern-day, TV-watching, churchgoing family and transport them back in time. The family, the Pilgrims, get on a ride at an amusement part that whisks them back through twenty centuries to the time of Jesus' life and ministry.

With the assistance of a five-year-old tour guide (who turns out to be an angel) and a narrating family pet (a dog named "Wisdom"), they, *and you,* travel through all the scenes presented in the Gospels. A special effort is made in the story retelling to appeal to the reader's five senses. It is hoped that you will be able to better imagine the sights, sounds, tastes, smells, and feelings of the first century Holy Land. And an extra special effort is made to appeal to your sixth sense—your spiritual awareness of Jesus' presence with you, now, in your twentieth-century world.

In case this is your first exposure to *The Bible Ride* series, there are some facts and figures you should be aware of before you join the Pilgrims for the last week of the tour.

The Main Characters

Mr. and Mrs. Pilgrim. These are the parents of Pete and Priscilla and the owners of Wisdom, the narrating dog-wonder. It can be assumed that they are "any parents" from the twentieth century, struggling to balance two kids, two jobs, two cars, and too much to do.

Priscilla Pilgrim. Priscilla is a seventh grader. She is precise, wears a wrist computer, and is really into facts. In fact, she is something of a female Jack Friday and no-nonsense scientist, all rolled into one.

Pete Pilgrim. Pete is Priscilla's seven-year-old younger brother. He is the shadow to her substance. Pete is a tightly wound bundle of id. Pete is into possibilities, risky adventures, feelings, and his tastebuds. Especially his tastebuds. Where Priscilla is cautious and calculating, Pete is three-sheets-to-the-wind hyperactivity.

Wisdom. Wisdom is the family dog. She's just a plain ole lovable dog—but with one exception. On this trip Wisdom is the narrator. You know that. The Pilgrims don't. Being a dog, Wisdom is able to report information with great attention to sights, sounds, and especially smells.

Jesna. Jesna is the tour guide. The Pilgrims had never met her before their family vacation at the amusement park, Daffy World. She is on hand to answer all the too-tough-to-handle questions that only Pete, and sometimes Priscilla, would dare to ask. Good thing she turns out to be an angel who has been running these tours for a millennium or two. But keep that quiet. The Pilgrims aren't sure about that just yet.

What Has Happened in the Previous Books?

In volumes one and two of *The Bible Ride* series, the Pilgrim family has traveled with Jesus through all the scenes of his life leading up to his last week on earth—Passion Week.

When volume three opens they are all back at the amusement park. It seems that there is a problem with the fine print of the conditions for being on the ride. You must want to stay with Jesus more than anything else in life.

The Pilgrims have all fallen head-over-heels in love with Jesus. And that's just the problem for Pete. Pete isn't sure he can stand to see what is about to happen. Jesna has suggested that he (they all) travel back to Daffy World and wait—until Pete knows that he can stomach the events of Passion Week.

So volume three opens with the Pilgrims back at the park. But Jesna is nowhere to be found!

A Few Rules for Time Travel

The Pilgrims' thirty-three-year trip through the scenes of the Gospels will be completed in sixty earth-seconds. This proves very convenient since Pete has rarely gone over five minutes without having to eat a snack or go to the bathroom.

In taking the ride, the Pilgrims become holograms. They can hear (Jesna has set the control panel for "English"), and enjoy their other four senses. However, they do, as holograms, have a feature that angels apparently enjoy—traveling through walls and mountainsides without a problem.

With that said, grab hold of your cart. The ride will begin when you turn the next page. I hope that the sixty scenes that follow will heighten your passion and joy for the good news of Jesus with, and in, you.

THE BEST NEWS YET

Jesna had vanished! My doggy nose was working double time to find her, but there wasn't even a trace of her sweet scent anywhere.

Pete was the first human to notice. His head was still bobbing around as if he were a bewildered chicken when the other Pilgrims realized their five-year-old tour guide was no longer guiding.

"OK, let's all stay calm," Mr. Pilgrim said. "She told us she might not be our guide anymore. But I bet she's just checking in with her boss or something."

"We just left her boss—back in Jerusalem," Priscilla moaned. "And if Petey hadn't gotten so squeamish, we'd still be with both of them right now!"

"Well, I couldn't help it," Pete snapped. "Those mean men were about to nail Jesus to a cross. You know I'm not allowed to watch horror movies! And, besides, it wasn't no movie! It was realer than the zit on your face."

"OK, OK, that'll be enough of that," Mr. Pilgrim said. "All the bickering doesn't bring Jesna back."

"Or get us back to Jerusalem," Priscilla added, ignoring her father's "stop-right-now-or-else" look.

"We'll need to spread out and look for her," Mr. Pilgrim continued. "You'll come with me, Son. And we'll all meet back here in ten minutes. With those little legs of hers she couldn't have gone far."

"Ten earth minutes?" Pete questioned.

"Yes, Son. Earth minutes."

"Then come with me, Dad," Pete shouted as he took his

father by the hand and pulled him toward the cross-shaped opening in the wooden fence. "Let's go back through the gate. I bet she's in there. Just like you said—talking to her boss."

Pete took three quick steps toward the cross of light shining through the weathered fence and then one giant bounce back to the ground—as if he had been trying to dart through a closed refrigerator.

"Ouch!!! Hey, what was that?"

Mrs. Pilgrim quickly knelt by her son to inspect his head. I joined them and gave Pete a sympathetic whimper and a tail wag. I was expecting to see his forehead sprout a cartoon-sized knot myself. Mr. Pilgrim was still standing in front of the "opening" to the Bible Ride. He began to slide his hands over the invisible barrier that had sent Pete sprawling. He looked like a mime trapped in a box (even though his face wasn't that white).

"Well, if this isn't something," Mr. Pilgrim mused.

"Careful, Dad," Priscilla warned. "It might be a force field."

"It *is* a forced field," Pete quipped while struggling to his feet. "It forced me to sit down here in what used to be a field."

After a few more minutes of head scratching and miming, Mr. Pilgrim said, "It's no use. It's sealed tight as a drum."

"So what can we do, Dad?" Priscilla asked. "We didn't even get a chance to say goodbye to Jesna."

"Or to see if we could adopt her," Pete added, glancing up at his mom with a hopeful grin.

"I think you should stay here with Pete now, Dear," Mr. Pilgrim said to his wife. "Prissy and I will take a quick look around."

"And bring some hot dogs back, Dad," Pete added.

As the other three Pilgrims gave Pete a look of disbelief, he explained, "Jesna said that I should come back to the park and eat some hot dogs before deciding to go back or not."

"She didn't say a *thing* about hot dogs, Pete," Priscilla snapped. "And how you can think about food at a time like this is beyond me."

I decided to tag along with Mr. Pilgrim and Priscilla. It had been a long time since I had seen any humans who weren't wearing robes and riding (and smelling like) donkeys. I was curious to see if they would seem the same after our thirty-three-year (sixty-earth-seconds) adventure.

A brisk ten-minute scouting trip proved disappointing. Our whirlwind tour through the park produced lots of smells but no Jesna. And, even after a thirty-three-Bible-years' absence, modern amusement-park humans seemed about the same as New Testament cousins—just less furry. You can clip a poodle, I guess, but there's still a dog inside.

Mr. Pilgrim and Priscilla returned with downcast heads and full hands. Each was carrying an oversized hot dog for Pete—who was still propped against the fence by the entrance to the Bible Ride.

Pete reached up and took the two greasy presents—one in each hand—never questioning that both were intended for his belly. He eagerly took a bite of the "dog" (an unfortunate choice of words, I've always thought) in his right hand. A few moments of loud chewing and unsightly sights followed. Then I heard the most unexpected words that had ever traveled into my doggy ears.

"Uh, does somebody want to finish these?" Pete asked. "I seem to have lost my appetite. It's hard to think about anything except how much I want to be back between the covers of the Bible with Jesus. I think he might need me."

The three older Pilgrims stared down at Pete in wide-mouthed astonishment.

"Amazing," Mrs. Pilgrim said.

"Unbelievable," Mr. Pilgrim followed.

"It's the end of the world," said Priscilla.

"Nope," said a small, angelic-sounding voice. "It's only the beginning."

"Jesna!!!" sang the Pilgrim quartet. "Where have you been?!"

"Just waiting for Pete to decide if being with Jesus was what he wanted more than anything else in the universe—even if being with him will be very painful."

"Oh, it is what I want!" Pete said.

"Then let's get back on the ride," Jesna chirped.

Pete was the first to bolt through the cross of light—taking it by faith that the invisible refrigerator he had crashed into before had been moved. And, even though I was bringing up the rear, I could hear Pete say to Jesna, "Hey! We made it. That is one way-cool door!"

SCENE 181
JESUS' DEATH IS PREMEDITATED[1]

When we arrived back in Bible time, it was two days before the Passover Feast. The temple courtyard was already abuzz with people. *Ah,* I thought while breathing in deeply, *it's good to get away from the smell of modern cologne—back to the aroma of old spices.*

"Jesus!" Pete cried out, just nanoseconds from hurling himself over the side of the car and breaking into a run. Arriving at Jesus' side, he continued, "Boy, did I miss you! I couldn't even get a whole hot dog down. Can you believe it? I thought I'd better get back here and look after you...."

Jesus turned toward Pete's mouth-in-motion and gave him a quick wink. It went undetected by the crowd of listeners but lit a glow in Pete's eyes. He snuggled up under Jesus' right arm as he continued to teach the people.

"So," Priscilla whispered to Jesna, "it must be April 12, A.D. 29, since it's two days before Passover and the calendar is four years off."

"That's exactly right, Priscilla," Jesna said.

"Well," Priscilla continued, "I can't think of a better place to be on this day."

"Me neither," Pete mumbled up through Jesus' sleeve. "And I don't want any of you to worry about Jesus none. I'll make sure he doesn't get hurt. They'll have to come through me first. I knew those two karate lessons would come in handy someday."

"Talk about your goldfish protecting an aircraft carrier," Priscilla whispered as she nudged Jesna in the ribs.

But Jesna didn't laugh. She just smiled a sad smile.

"I was just thinking, though," Priscilla went on. "Things

were really getting hot for Jesus before we went back. Do you think it *really is* safe for him to be out in public like this, with such a large crowd gathered around?"

"No!" Jesna responded. "It's not safe at all. But this is how Jesus has chosen to spend his time before the famous Passover meal he'll share with his disciples. For the past few days he's been camping out with them at night—on the Mount of Olives—and then teaching each day in the temple."

"Well, his popularity with the people really seems to be growing."

"With *some* of the people, Priscilla. But not with others. Come on. I need to show you what I mean."

With a "come-along" hand motion from Jesna, Pete slipped away from Jesus and joined us as we followed Jesna across the temple courtyard.

"Where we going?" Pete asked.

"To the palace of the high priest," Jesna answered somberly.

"You mean priests have palaces? I thought just kings and Herods had palaces."

"Not all the priests have palaces, Pete. Just the high priest."

"The real tall ones?"

"No, Pete," Jesna giggled.

"The boss priest?"

"Umm, yeah, sort of, Pete."

"Well, that seems a little odd to me, too," Mr. Pilgrim said as we continued to slip and dodge our way over the crowded sandstone.

Jesna explained. "You see, Mr. Pilgrim, for the past hundred years or so, since the Romans took over, the high priests have been appointed by Rome—as are all the civil leaders (like Herod). They still come from Aaron's descendants, but ..."

"They're working for a different boss?"

"Ah-humph," Jesna laughed. "I guess you could say it that way, Mr. Pilgrim. That sure seems to be true for the current boss priest, Caiaphas."

Our walk to Caiaphas' palace, atop Mount Zion, took us a few hundred yards outside the city walls. The last steps of the hike were across a small courtyard surrounded on all four sides by beautiful archways, two stories high, and hanging green plants. We then crept through (and I do mean right through) a thick wooden door. The room we entered was alive with loud conversation. Fortunately, there weren't any cats around to distract me from paying close attention to the priests—high and low.

"We've got to do something about Jesus!" a man with dark, curly hair and earrings said above the noise. "He keeps performing signs and miracles. If we don't put a stop to it *everyone* will start to believe in him, and the Romans will march in and take away everything we've worked for."

Then a man wearing a silky black robe stood to his feet. The noise level in the room suddenly receded into silence. A nearby candle lit up the white specks in his beard and a big blue vein in the center of his forehead.

"That's Caiaphas," Jesna whispered.

"So this is his mansion," Pete said while nodding his furrowed chin. "The priest's done good."

"You know nothing at all!" Caiaphas shouted while pointing an angry finger at the one who had just spoken. "Don't you know anything? Can't you see that it's to our advantage that one man dies for the people rather than the whole nation be destroyed?"[2]

At that Pete let out a yell and crouched into a karate position. I knew just how he felt. I wanted to bite the man myself, but Jesna reached over and restrained Pete from attacking Caiaphas' midsection. Then she said, "It's OK, Pete. You can holster those hands now. Jesus' Dad has everything under control."

Pete shot her a puzzled look.

Jesna responded, "He just caused Rome's head priest to unknowingly prophesy that Jesus will sacrificially die for the nation, and not only the nation, but also so that God's exile-scattered children might be gathered together into one people. He just prophesied that what Jesus is about to do will someday make it possible for a little suburb-living, karate-kicking Pete to find his way back to his spiritual home."

That seemed to satisfy Pete. He let his two lethal weapons rest by his side.

FAMILY DISCUSSION

1. Do you ever feel like doing something really brave to help Jesus?
2. What is the best thing you could do for him tomorrow?

SCENE 182
THE BETRAYAL BY JUDAS[3]

Whoosh!

"Hey!" Pete cried. "Why don't you watch where you're going? You ran right through me."

The blur of robe and hair that had swept into the room (and through Pete and me) stopped in front of the still-standing Caiaphas. When he turned and knelt we could see who it was. Judas.

"What's he doing here?" Pete asked. "I've had a bad feeling about him ever since he scolded Jesus for letting that woman make his feet smell better. He's looked funny—in the eyes—ever since."

"Well, the eyes are the windows to the soul, Son," Mrs. Pilgrim said.

"Then he's had his shades down for some time now," Pete said.

"Shhhh," Priscilla said. "I want to hear this."

Judas straightened up from his prolonged bow and cleared his throat to speak. "Most holy Caiaphas," he began.

"Kiss-up!" Pete blurted out.

Priscilla shushed him again.

"I know the man you were just talking about," Judas continued.

"We all know that. We've seen you with him. You're one of his followers," Caiaphas hissed.

"I am Judas, Judas of Kerioth. I have been with Jesus of Nazareth for three years. I confess to you that I thought he was the one whom the prophets described—the Messiah."

A rumble began to boil in the room.

"But," Judas said in a loud voice, "I was wrong. He is powerless to establish a lasting kingdom on this earth." Judas cast his gaze to the floor. "He is a false messiah, and I am a fool who has wasted three years following him."

"Why are you telling us what we already know, Judas?" a voice asked from the darkness.

"Do you want this man?" Judas asked, his eyes still downcast.

"Yes!" was the loud response of many voices.

"What will you give me if I hand him over to you?"

Caiaphas took a couple of steps to his right and bent over. We could all hear the high-pitched sound of metal jingling as he withdrew his hands from a wooden chest. He turned to face Judas. Candlelight reflected from a mound of silver coins he held in his cupped hands.

"How does thirty pieces of silver sound to you?"

Judas reached inside his robe and pulled out a leather pouch. He held it open to receive Caiaphas' deposit. He said no more, gave a nod to the high priest, and walked away.

An eerie yellow light shone from Judas' eyes as he passed back through us on his way out of the room. I shook myself from tail to nose to get rid of the creepy feeling that gave me.

"Ooooh," Pete said as Judas was walking out the doorway. "Did you see his eyes? That was scary."

"I saw it, Pete," Jesna said. "It looked like the shades were up and the prince of this world had moved in."

"Well," Caiaphas' voice boomed out in self-satisfied tones, "does that not prove we are doing work that will bring a smile to the face of God?"

"The face of *your* god," Jesna snapped, "was on each of the coins you gave Judas—the face of Caesar."

FAMILY DISCUSSION

1. How could it be that Caiaphas, a boss priest, missed the true identity of Jesus?
2. What do you think Judas loved more than Jesus?
3. What do you think Judas was feeling as he left the room?

SCENE 183
PREPARATION FOR THE PASSOVER[4]

We camped out for the night on the Mount of Olives along with Jesus and his disciples. Judas was there too—acting as if *nothing* had happened at the high priest's house! When Pete saw Judas sitting at the campfire with Jesus, it took all the restraint Mr. and Mrs. Pilgrim could muster to keep Pete from punching the traitor in the stomach. To be honest, I flashed my teeth at the man a few times myself.

At one point, Judas went away and Jesus continued teaching his disciples. Pete managed to calm down a little as he listened. Priscilla wondered aloud, "Do you think Jesus feels badly about not getting through to Judas?"

"Yeah," Pete replied. "He hooked twelve fish, but it looks like one—the slimiest—got away."

"That reminds me of something I heard a preacher say," Mr. Pilgrim interjected, launching into his story before anyone else could comment on Priscilla's question. "He said that when he first started preaching he was having a tough time with one of his deacons. Things got so bad, he went back to his seminary to ask his favorite professor what he should do about it. And do you know what his professor said?"

"No, Dad, you were the one who heard the sermon. I was probably eating cookies in the church basement."

"Well, Pete, he said, 'Don't worry about it. Even Jesus had problems holding on to one of his first twelve. And, knowing you as well as I do, *you* should be happy to catch *one* out of every twelve.'"

"Ouch!" Mrs. Pilgrim said. "I'd hate to hear what that professor said to the students he *didn't* like."

"No, no. He liked that student. They stayed best of friends. His point was, well, his point was …"

"Perhaps," Jesna inserted, "that with the world, the flesh, and the devil to fight against, making true disciples is a tough job."

"Yep, sure is," Pete said assuredly. "Shoot, I'm not so sure this disciplin' would be working on *me* if I weren't spending all this time with Jesus. But I still want to bite Judas."

Me too, I growled to myself.

It wasn't long until Passover began. The next day—the first

day of the "Feast of Unleavened Bread" is what Jesna called it—Jesus motioned for Peter and John to come away from the campsite (on the Mount of Olives) for a private talk. Pete insisted that Jesus wouldn't mind if we listened in.

"I want you to go and prepare the Passover for us so we can eat it together," Jesus said to them.

Peter and John replied, "Where do you want us to do this?"

Jesus said, "Keep your eyes open as you enter the city. A man carrying a water jug will meet you. Follow him home. Then speak with the owner of the house: 'The Teacher wants to know,

Where is the hallway where I can eat the Passover meal with my disciples?' He will show you a spacious second-story room, swept and ready. Prepare the meal there."

And with that the disciples were off—with us driving along behind.

As we traveled, Priscilla said, "Jesna, I've been thinking."

"Uh-oh," Pete blurted out. "Every time you do that you weaken the nation."

"Shut up, little brother. As I was saying, you know how much Jesus likes to communicate with pictures and symbols—more than with words, it seems sometimes?"

"Yes," Jesna said.

"Like," Priscilla continued, "it's almost as if he and his Father were making a movie and every scene is important and means even more than you think it does when you first see it."

"Yeah," Jesna said in a "please-go-on" tone.

"Well," Priscilla continued quietly, reverently, "this is the day that fathers, all over the country, are killing Passover lambs. Right?"

"Yeah, and it's gross!" Pete inserted.

"That's right, Priscilla," Jesna said. "That's done *now* to commemorate how God delivered his people from Egypt and established Israel as a nation, in the land—the kingdom—he had promised to Abraham."

"But I still don't know why all the lamb killing has to be done," Pete said adamantly.

"The lambs, Pete, were killed—the first time—as a sacrifice to God and so the blood could be used to mark the doorways so that God's angels would know that his children lived inside."

"Well, tonight," Priscilla inserted, "I wonder if Jesus is about to start a new tradition, one where he's the *new* lamb that has to die."

"Wow!" said Mr. Pilgrim. "I never thought about it just like that before."

"And I don't want to think about *that* again," Pete pouted.

"But," Jesna followed, "what Priscilla is saying is exactly why Jesus wanted you all to come on this ride—so you could get a fresh look, a deeper look, at the Gospels he wrote with his life.

"Now that you're taking the time to get to know him with your hearts," she continued while giving Priscilla a nod, "you'll see tonight how Jesus wants you to begin commemorating a whole *new* Passover where *he* is the lamb. He'll even show you how to begin marking your hearts with his lamb's blood to let all the angels in heaven (and demons in hell) know that he lives inside his children."

FAMILY DISCUSSION

1. What is the significance to you, personally, of Jesus being your Passover Lamb?
2. Did you know that when people take Communion (the Eucharist) they are carrying on the tradition of a Passover meal?

3. How does it make you feel—deep down inside—to know that when you take Communion you are marking the doorpost of your heart with the blood of Jesus?

SCENE 184
WASHING THE DISCIPLES' FEET[5]

"Jesna?"

"Yes, Priscilla."

"I've been wondering. What Jesus just said to Peter and John was a little confusing. He told them to go and ask for a 'hallway,' so they could have Passover together."

"Yes, go on."

"Well, then he said, 'He will show you a spacious second-story room, swept and ready.' Are they the same thing, 'hallway' and 'upstairs room'?"

"Priscilla, you never miss a thing."

"You get used to it after a while," Pete said with a frown.

"The word that Jesus used, 'hallway,' means—in this culture—the place in a house where beasts of burden are unloaded and shoes and dusty garments put down. The only other time that word is used in the Gospels is to designate the place in Bethlehem where Jesus was born."[6]

"That sounds like a pretty humble request," Mr. Pilgrim said.

"Exactly," said Jesna. "Jesus told them to ask for a lowly place. After all, if it was good enough for his birth, it would be good enough for celebrating the Passover with his friends. But," she continued, "he also told them that the owner of the house would offer a choice room. Probably one that had been prepared for his own family."

"Wow," Priscilla said. "The owner of that house must be a secret disciple."

"I'm sure you are right, Priscilla. Undoubtedly he is one of the many who have been influenced by Jesus' sermons."

"Influenced enough to start acting humbly, like a true follower of Jesus, it sounds like to me," Mrs. Pilgrim inserted.

"Exactly! And, Priscilla, you're about to witness another example of the humility Jesus wants us to imitate. You'll see after we get there."

It wasn't long before Peter and John returned from their errand with the exciting news. All had gone just as Jesus said it would. We proceeded to follow along behind Jesus and his friends as they walked the streets of Jerusalem, arriving at a medium-sized house.

A man with brightly smiling eyes met our party at the door and ushered Jesus and his friends across the dusty "hallway" which had been requested by Peter and John.

He then led the way up a narrow flight of stone stairs and into a large room. The floor of the room was tiled with smooth rocks, and the walls were covered with a brown, sandy plaster. Late-afternoon light shone in through two square windows and lit up a long rectangular table in the middle of the room. The wooden table was very low to the ground and was surrounded on three sides by a "U" of couches.

"Psst, Jesna," Pete whispered. "I wonder if that man knows what's going on here. I mean, if he tells one of the disciples his name he could become famous for this."

"Look at the smile in his eyes, Pete. He's already got all the good feelings a heart can hold. That's what happens when you start acting like Jesus—giving up the best place to someone in need."

As the happy host left the room, Jesus had a big smile on his face, too.

Jesus then motioned with his hands for the disciples to be seated around the table. (Actually, they were kind of *lying* around the table on the couches, propped up on their elbows so they could eat without spilling anything.) Jesus himself took a spot between John (on his right) and Judas (on his left). Judas looked very troubled, as if it were more than his body he couldn't get comfortable.

"Wow!" Pete said. "I feel all warm and tingly inside. I've never felt like this before."

"Yes," Priscilla echoed. "And I feel like I'm standing on the canvas of a famous painting."

They weren't the only ones feeling that way. I thought my heart was going to be permanently stretched by warm feelings—and I'm a dog.

After the last couch was adjusted, a long minute of reverence sealed the lips of the disciples and pushed Judas' head toward the floor.

The holy hush was broken when Jesus rose from his couch and walked to a corner of the room. He set aside his outer robe and put on an apron that had been lying on a wooden bench. He then poured water from a large earthen pot into a basin and dipped a thick white cloth into the water.

When the cloth was saturated Jesus turned and walked back toward the disciples at the table. Three drops of holy water fell from the soaked fabric and made tiny wet circles on the rock floor. They sparkled with rays borrowed from the evening sun.

Jesus stopped at the table and began to wash one of the disciples' feet. The other disciples exchanged startled looks. When Jesus dried those same feet with the apron, ten heads began shaking "no." (Judas' head didn't move, though. His eyes were glued to his own feet.)

Jesus was unfazed by the shock waves that were passing over his bowed head. But when he went on and knelt at the dusty feet of Simon Peter, the brash disciple blurted out, "Master, are *you* going to wash *my* feet?"

Jesus answered, "I know you don't understand what I'm doing, but it will be clear to you later."

Peter stood to his dirty feet and said emphatically, "You are not going to wash my feet—ever!"

Jesus looked up at him from the position of a servant and said, "If I don't wash you, you can't take part in what I'm doing."

"Then, Master," Peter said, "not only my feet but my hands and my head!"

Jesus began to wash Peter's feet as he said, "He who has bathed does not need to wash except for his feet; then he is clean all over; and (now) you are clean all over. But," Jesus continued as he stood to his feet, "not each of you; you are not all clean."

When Jesus said that, Judas dropped his head even lower. It was so low even a dog could see its crown—which, I am sure, would be the only one he would ever wear.

When Jesus had finished washing all twenty-four feet—including those of the traitor—he put his outer robe back on and went back to his place at the table.

A few moments passed in silence before the only man left with dirty feet in the room said in a serious voice,

> "Do you understand what I have done to you? You address me as 'Teacher' and 'Master,' and rightly so. That is what I am. So if I, the Master and Teacher, washed your feet, you

must now wash each other's feet. I've laid down a pattern for you. What I've done, you do. I'm only pointing out the obvious. A servant is not ranked above his master; an employee doesn't give orders to the employer. If you understand what I'm telling you, act like it—and live a blessed life."[7]

As Jesus spoke those words my dog ears picked up a faint wood-on-stone sound from the first floor of the house. I don't know how many of the disciples understood Jesus' object lesson, but the homeowner was already living it. He was preparing another room so his family could celebrate the Passover meal, and he was, no doubt, living a blessed life.

FAMILY DISCUSSION

1. What do you think Judas was feeling when Jesus washed his feet?
2. What are some ways (which don't involve water and feet) that you can imitate the example of Jesus, as a servant, tomorrow?

SCENE 185

JESUS FORETELLS HIS BETRAYAL[8]

The two windows in the upper room began to glow with the rich orange and red hues of a fiery sunset. Candles, lit much earlier by the host, began to make their presence known as daylight faded.

Jesus stood and walked over to one of the windows. He stared out intently.

"What's Jesus doing?" Pete asked. "This is a strange time to be watching the sun set."

"He's watching for the first signs that it is time to begin the Feast of Unleavened Bread," Jesna answered.

"Well, how will he know? Skywriting?"

"Exactly, Pete."

"Huh?"

"The feast begins when the first three stars are visible in the evening sky. Their appearance is confirmed by a threefold blast from silver trumpets—from the Temple Mount."

"Wow!" Pete said. "Awesome!"

"I wonder if there is some significance in the three stars and the three star-watchers that came to Bethlehem from the east?" Priscilla thought out loud.

"You scare me, Sis," Pete said.

"You amaze me, Priscilla," Jesna said as she reached over and placed her hand inside Priscilla's.

At that moment Jesus turned from the window and began walking back toward the table. Three long trumpet cheers pierced the evening air. It was God's time for the feast to begin.

Jesus took his place and began to serve his disciples.

During their meal, Jesus said, "I have something very difficult but important to say to you: One of you is going to hand me over to the enemies of the kingdom."

Eleven of the disciples seemed stunned, as if they had been hit on the head with a stick. One began to inspect his feet.

The eleven began to ask Jesus, one after the other, "It isn't me, is it, Master?"

Jesus answered,

> "The one who hands me over is someone I eat with daily, one who passes me food at the table. [He glanced to his left.] In one sense the Son of Man is entering into a way of treachery well-marked by the Scriptures—no surprises here.

In another sense that man who turns him in, turns traitor to the Son of Man—better never to have been born than do this!"[9]

At that Judas sprang to his feet. Terror flashed from his eyes as he—the last to ask—blurted out, "It isn't me, is it, Rabbi?"

Jesus stood up and looked directly at Judas, compassion welling in his eyes. "Don't play any more games with me, Judas," is all that Jesus said.

Perhaps for the first time in many months, Judas took the words of Jesus to heart. He bolted out of the room and into the arms of darkness—clutching his money pouch as he ran.

FAMILY DISCUSSION

1. Do you think Jesus still loved Judas—even though he had done something so horrible?
2. What do you think it was that Judas loved more than Jesus? Why?

SCENE 186

THE LAST SUPPER[10]

Jesus remained standing for a while. He looked very sad. It seemed to take all of his resolve to keep from racing after Judas. Such are the instincts of a Good Shepherd.

Shoot! If I thought I could've pulled it off, I would have herded Judas back myself.

But I knew what Jesus knew. Judas had already sold his soul to the wolf.

Jesus lowered himself again to his couch. A deep silence fell over the room, as if time itself had stopped to watch what was about to happen.

Then Jesus reached and picked up a flat circle of bread. He broke it. A few crumbs fell to the table. They glowed in the warm candlelight.

He gave the broken bread to his disciples and said:

> "Take, eat. This is my body."

The disciples seemed puzzled but obeyed their master.

After each had eaten a piece of the bread, Jesus lifted a clay cup from the table. He whispered a prayer of thanks while looking up toward his Father, then passed the cup to John. As the disciple looked at Jesus with puzzled eyes, Jesus said:

> "Drink this, all of you. This is my blood, God's new covenant poured out for many people for the forgiveness of sins."

As the first disciple drank from the cup, Jesus continued:

> "I'll not be drinking wine from this cup again until that new day when I'll drink with you in the kingdom of my Father."[11]

After the cup had been passed and each disciple had drunk in the new covenant, another holy silence filled the room. It was broken by Simon Peter's baritone voice leading the way through a hymn.

As they sang by candlelight, I noticed Pete rubbing his eyes and then shaking his head. But he didn't speak.

When the singing stopped, Jesus and his friends began to file out of the room. The first Communion service in the history of the world had come to a close. Passover would never be the same.

"So," Priscilla said reverently, "that's what Jesus meant

months ago when he said, 'I am the living bread which came down from heaven.'"

"That's right," Jesna whispered back. "And he also said, 'If anyone eats this bread, he will live forever; and the bread which I shall give for the life of the world is my flesh.'"

Mr. and Mrs. Pilgrim nodded their understanding as the family quietly followed Jesna out of the room.

Pete was slowly bringing up the rear. Before he walked out of the doorway, however, he bent down and put his arm around my back and talked quietly into my ear.

"I know everyone else will think I'm crazy, girl, but while the singing was going on, I think I saw an angel or something. Two angels. It was a foggy picture, but I saw an old man untying a boy—about Priscilla's size—and helping him down from a pile of rocks. Then they both knelt down and stared at Jesus and started crying. Pretty weird, huh? Don't tell Priscilla. She already thinks I'm nuts."

I wasn't going to tell. I was just glad I wasn't the only one that saw it.

Pete stood up. But instead of continuing through the doorway, he walked back over to the table where Jesus had served his friends. He brushed some bread crumbs into his tiny hand and slowly emptied his palm into his mouth.

His parents poked their heads back through the doorway just in time to see him. From the tears sliding down their faces I think they knew it wasn't his stomach Pete was trying to feed. They looked at him as if he were a vision; or as if he were Isaac—spared by a lamb.

FAMILY DISCUSSION

1. Why do you think Pete ate crumbs from the table where Jesus had served his disciples?

2. What do you think Jesus meant when he said he was the "bread of life"?
3. Are you taking in enough of Jesus to keep your spiritual life alive and healthy?

SCENE 187
THE NEW COMMANDMENT OF LOVE[12]

We caught up with Jesus and his friends as they were passing through the city gate that led to the Mount of Olives. No one was talking. Each disciple was staring at his feet—as if not wanting to know what was ahead. Jesus kept his gaze on the horizon. Perhaps he wanted to see beyond what lay ahead.

The slow-paced march came to a halt at the campsite. Two of the disciples began to build a fire. There was a chill in the April air, and in everyone's January hearts.

As a fire slowly came to life, Jesus sat by it—cross-legged on the ground. His face was to Jerusalem. The holy city glowed with the light of a thousand torches. Above him was a clear night sky. Ten thousand stars had an unblocked view of their Maker.

The closest cluster of olive trees stood behind Jesus, their leaves at a safe distance from the tiny orange spaceships being launched by the fire.

When the last of the eleven disciples had taken a seat, Jesus began to talk.

> "Children, I am with you for only a short time longer. You are going to look high and low for me. But just as I told the Jews, I'm telling you: 'Where I go, you are not able to come.'"

Pete shot his father a startled look. Then Jesus continued:

"Let me give you a new command: Love one another. In the same way I loved you, you love one another. This is how everyone will recognize that you are my disciples—when they see the love you have for each other."[13]

Pete was still waiting for his father to answer the questioning look he had sent him. Finally Pete blurted out, "Where's Jesus going, and why can't we get there from here?"

"He's going back home to be with his Father," Jesna answered. "And you can go there. Just not right now."

"Well, how do *I* get there from here?" Pete asked.

"By obeying his new command. By loving others in the same way he loves you."

"Well, is there a shortcut to heaven, then?" Pete asked seriously. "Because I don't think I can make it on that road."

"Oh, *you* can't," Jesna said.

"Huh?" sang the Pilgrim quartet.

"You'd have a better chance of crossing the desert wilderness between Egypt and Israel—without any food and without a compass—than you would of making it to heaven on your own."

"Then it's impossible!" Pete moaned.

"No," Jesna said while smiling, "it's easy. The Israelites didn't have to cross the desert without food—they were given manna. And they had a compass—a cloud by day and a pillar of fire at night.

"And you," she continued, "have even more advantages in making it across the wilderness of earth-life. Jesus himself is your new 'manna.' (You've already eaten some, Pete. Back at the upper room.) And soon he'll send a much better compass—his Holy Spirit—to guide you."

"So," Pete began, "if you have Jesus inside you and his

Holy Spirit as a guide, you can't miss heaven."

"Not quite that simple, Pete. You also have to be willing to imitate the example of Jesus' final parable on earth—obedience unto death."

Pete looked very sad. He stared at the ground and slowly shook his head from side to side. "I'll never be able to love that much."

"You don't have to," Jesna said.

"What?" rang the second verse from the Pilgrim singers.

"You just have to be willing to let Jesus do it through you. And that's as different from doing it yourself as day is from night."

"Or as Jesus is from a Pharisee?" Pete asked through a smile.

"Exactly," said Jesna.

FAMILY DISCUSSION

1. Why don't you make a list of at least three things you can do tomorrow—for each member of your family—that will cause them to feel loved by you?
2. Take a moment for silent prayer. Ask Jesus which one thing on your list (for each of your family members) he would like for you to do. Then ask him to help you do it.

SCENE 188
PETER'S DENIAL PREDICTED[14]

The campfire had reached its full stature. A couple of the disciples inched away from its heat. Jesus sat still. The fire was painting his face with a warm orange glow.

Then he told them,

> "Before the night's over, you're going to fall to pieces because of what happens to me. There is a Scripture that says, 'I'll strike the shepherd; helter-skelter the sheep will be scattered.' But after I am raised up, I, your Shepherd, will go ahead of you, leading the way to Galilee."[15]

Simon Peter blurted out, "Even if each of these falls away on account of you, Lord, I won't."

Jesus looked over at his spunky disciple. His eyes quickly filled with water. When he blinked, a lone tear slid down his cheek and got lost in his beard.

The disciple turned his head to face Jesus' tear-streaked countenance. Half of Peter's face was red with firelight and hot emotion. Half was lost in dark shadow.

Jesus finally spoke. "Don't be so sure about what will come out of your mouth, Peter. Because I know, this very night, before the rooster crows at dawn, you will deny me three times."

"No!" Peter protested loudly. "Even if everyone here falls to pieces on account of you, I won't!"

Jesus stared back at the fire as a ten-voice chorus of disciples sang their allegiance to Jesus.

"It doesn't compute," Priscilla interrupted. "How could anyone who has seen as much as these disciples have ever deny Jesus? That would be like Columbus denying that there is wind, after it had pushed him across the Atlantic."

"Yeah," Pete said, trying to get into the act with his big sister. "It would be like a rhinoceros denying there's a big ole ugly spike sticking out of its head. Or like ..."

"We get the point, Pete," said Mrs. Pilgrim.

"I just don't know how Jesus' best friends could ever deny him—especially not Peter!" Priscilla continued.

"I know, I know," Jesna began. "But you have to remember that even the people who understand Jesus best still have earth eyes and not heaven eyes."

"What's that?" Mr. Pilgrim asked.

"Earth eyes? That means they still see almost everything from their perspective in the tangible world. Down deep inside most of them are still expecting Jesus to set up a physical kingdom here on earth. Even though they've been hearing Jesus talk about his Father's spiritual kingdom for three years now, they don't see it clearly yet. They don't see with heaven eyes.

"Plus," Jesna continued, "they haven't stared into the faces of an angry mob of men who plan to kill them either. And when Peter does—as he will before morning—he will realize that many pockets of his heart are still filled with fear instead of love."

"So," Priscilla said slowly, "it takes heaven eyes and a heart completely filled with love to pass the most difficult tests."

"That's right, Priscilla," Jesna answered. "Love is the glue that holds hearts—and groups of disciples—together."

"Well, I want me some of them glasses from heaven and a big ole drum of that heart glue stuff!" Pete announced. "I don't want to go to pieces when things get tough following Jesus."

"Don't worry for a moment, Pete," Jesna said. "You're on course to have a heart full and overflowing with love. And your glasses are being prepared as we speak."

"Good," Pete said. "And after I get those glasses, maybe I can see good enough to help Peter find him a pair. And then we'll really kick some b—"

"Pete!"

"Bad guys, Mom. What did you think?"

FAMILY DISCUSSION

1. How do you think Peter felt when Jesus said he would deny him three times before sunup?"
2. How do you think Jesus felt?
3. Are there any ways that you pretend not to know Jesus? If you answered "yes," this would be a great time to ask him for some more heart glue and special glasses.

SCENE 189

THE TWO SWORDS[16]

Simon Peter was still shaking his head in disbelief when Jesus began speaking again.

"You all remember when I sent you out with no purse or bag or sandals?"

Each disciple began to nod a "yes."

"He's talking about their internship, isn't he?" Priscilla asked no one in particular.

"Yes," Jesna whispered.

"Did you lack for anything?" Jesus asked the group.

"Nothing," one said. "Not a one of us lacked for anything."

"Well, in many ways, things are different now," Jesus said with steely-eyed seriousness. "When you go out on your own again, many will see you as criminals—because you were with me. The road ahead will be full of trouble. You must prepare yourself. You must look to what you need. You will all discover that a sword will be more important to you than a coat."

Then one said proudly, "Look, Master, two swords right here!"

"Wow!" Pete exclaimed. "He's going to teach 'em all how to sword fight before he, uh, leaves. I bet he's better than Zorro with a sword. I bet he could shave a 'J' in Zorro's whiskers before Zorro could get his sword out of its, uh, its, uh, sword-holder-thing."

And with that Pete grabbed up a long, straight stick and began to fence with his unarmed sister.

"Ouch. Stop that, you little pest."

"Whoa there, Pete," Jesna cautioned. "If Jesus had wanted to give the world the twelve musketeers, he wouldn't have waited this long to start training them. Plus, he'd probably have picked the twelve most muscular zealots instead of this odd assortment of skinny fishermen, dreamers, and one plump accountant."

"Well, you heard him say they had better sell their coats and buy some swords," Pete shot back while cutting small circles through the night air—inches from Priscilla's beet-red face.

"If you don't put that stick down I'm going to see how you like hot coals down your pants!" Priscilla said sternly.

Ka-thump! Pete's sword-stick hit the ground.

"Then wh-why did Jesus say that about having a sword?" Pete stammered from the safety of his mother's side.

"Because he wants his disciples to begin preparing for the trouble that lies ahead—while he's still with them."

"But he said, 'sword,'" Pete pouted. "I heard him!"

"Yes, Pete, you sure did," Jesna began. "Just as you heard him refer to his body as 'bread' and 'wine.'"

"And as a 'temple,'" Priscilla inserted.

"That's right, Priscilla. People with a vision of God's kingdom often use words with much deeper meaning than what we might first hear with, uh …"

"With our earth ears?"

"Yes, Pete. Exactly."

"So what is the 'sword' that Jesus wants them to defend themselves with?" Mr. Pilgrim asked.

"That's just what Jesus is about to explain to his friends," Jesna answered. "Listen."

As they did so, they could hear Jesus finishing up his sword talk. Then it was quiet.

The disciple who had proudly displayed the two swords was locked in a gaze with Jesus. As the silence continued, the disciple's face—which had been as energized as Pete's—slowly became somber. Then even that expression fell away when Jesus broke the silence.

"Enough of that; no more sword talk!"[17]

"Don't feel bad, Pete. The disciples have missed his meaning, too. But listen closely now. Jesus is going to make sure they understand just how to brandish the 'sword' of God's Spirit."

FAMILY DISCUSSION

1. How do you think the disciples felt when they heard Jesus talking about "swords" instead of "peace" and "love"?
2. Do you think Jesus was talking about "real" weapons or "spiritual" protection? Why do you think that?

SCENE 190

JESUS BEGINS HIS FAREWELL DISCOURSES: "LET NOT YOUR HEARTS BE TROUBLED"[18]

The disciple who had so proudly displayed the two swords retreated two paces. His face continued to reflect on Jesus' riddle as he rewrapped the dull metal swords with a dirt-stained cloth.

"Don't let this throw you," Jesus began. "You all trust in God, don't you? Then trust me. There is plenty of room for each of you in my Father's home. If that weren't so I wouldn't be telling you now that I am on my way to prepare rooms for each of you. That's what is happening now. I'm on my way to get your room ready. I'll come back soon and get you, so you can live where I have lived—and will live again."

At that point one of the disciples, Thomas, cleared his throat and proceeded to interrupt Jesus. "Master," he began, "we have no idea where you are going. How do you expect us to follow you?"

"That's ole Doubting Thomas, huh?" Pete asked.

"That's right," Jesna said.

"He probably doubts that he just saw two swords. I bet he's from Minnesota...."

"That's Missouri. Shhh!"

Jesus answered Thomas,

> "I am the Road, also the Truth, also the Life. No one gets to the Father apart from me. If you really knew me, you would know my Father as well. From now on, you do know him. You've even seen him!"[19]

"They've seen God because they've been living with Jesus. Isn't that right, Jesna?"

"Right again, Pete," Jesna answered. "They've been living with God—their Maker, the Creator of the entire universe—for the past three years. But most of them still don't *fully* comprehend that."

"'Cause if they really understood that they were already living on a nuclear-powered aircraft carrier, they wouldn't be thinking they needed a couple of swords to protect themselves, right, Jesna?"

"That's pretty amazing, Pete."

"Not really, Jesna. I've got you as a tour guide, and I was taught some of this stuff in Sunday school. Poor ole Thomas is having to learn it while it's all whizzing around him."

"You have a kind heart, Son."

"Thanks, Mom."

"Master," the disciple Philip said, "show us the Father; then we'll know what you mean."

"You've been with me all this time, Philip," Jesus began as his eyes were becoming shiny with moisture. "And you still don't understand?"

Jesus walked toward Philip and gently placed his hands on the shoulders of his thickheaded disciple. "To see me, Philip, is to see the Father. So how can you ask, 'Where is the Father?' Don't you believe that I am in the Father and the Father is in me? The Father lives in me and crafts each of my words into a divine act."

Philip tucked his head in shame.

Jesus turned his head to address all of his friends.

> "Believe me: I am in my Father and my Father is in me. If you can't believe that, believe what you see—these works. The person who trusts me will not only do what I'm doing but even greater things, because I, on my way to the Father, am giving you the same work to do that I've been doing. You can count on it. From now on, whatever you request along the lines of who I am and what I am doing, I'll do it. That's how the Father will be seen for who he is in the Son. I mean it. Whatever you request in this way, I'll do."[20]

"All right, Jesus!" Pete exclaimed. "Did you hear that, Mom? Jesus said whatever I wanted, all I have to do is ask him and he'll go get it for me!"

Mrs. Pilgrim immediately looked to Jesna for help. But it didn't come until Pete continued on.

"Let's see," Pete began as he latched on to a pinky in preparation for some serious counting. "First, I'll ask for a big-screen TV—so my new video games will look realer. Then I'll ask for more video games, and a new basketball, and a gym in my backyard to keep the basketball in, and a chocolate bar so big that even Jesus can't lift it—I'm sure he can get some angels to help, and...."

As Pete was starting in on the fingers of his other hand Jesna cleared her throat. "Ahhhhmmm."

"And I'll ask for new teeth that don't rot...."

"Ahhhhmmm."

"OK, OK, and I'll ask for some stuff for Priscilla, too, Jesna."

"Pete!" Jesna said in a surprisingly strong voice. "Pete! That was Jesus who made the promise, not Santa Claus. And he did not say I'll give you every pleasurable thing that you can possibly think of. He was saying that if you love God, you'll stay close to him and begin to imitate the good works that Jesus has done. Then, from that new position—snuggled up close to God—you can ask for whatever you want and expect to receive it."

"Yeah. So what's the catch?"

"There's no 'catch,' Pete. It's just that if you are so much in love with God that you want to keep constant company with him and love others like his Son Jesus does, well, then you'll be asking for things from a heart full of love—and, uh ..."

"And not from your growling stomach," Priscilla added indignantly.

"Oh," Pete said. "That's very different."

FAMILY DISCUSSION

1. Imagine that you were walking down a beach early one morning and found Aladdin's magic lamp. If you rubbed it and a genie came out, what would be three things you'd wish for?
2. Now imagine that you had been keeping constant company with Jesus for several weeks. You've come to see how he lives his life and how much he loves all of his children. You get all caught up in helping him help others. Then one night he asks you what you would like to ask for. What are your "wishes"?
3. How do your two lists compare?

SCENE 191

THE PROMISE OF HEAVEN'S HOLY HELPER[21]

Jesus returned to his seat by the fire. The disciple who had stood up to grab a sword and join the zealot militia reseated himself—ready to listen again to the Prince of Peace.

Jesus seemed very patient. He took time to look into the eyes of each of his friends before continuing. The fire seemed respectfully quiet. I don't think it popped once as it lit each face with a warm orange glow.

Jesna broke the silence with a hard sob.

From their positions as bookends, Priscilla and Mrs. Pilgrim slid an arm around her. Priscilla asked, "Are you OK, Jesna?"

"Oh yeah, I'll be fine. This part of the ride always gets to me. They've spent most of the last three years together—almost every minute of it. Now they only have a few hours left. And," she sobbed, "he's got so much love for his dear friends, he's going to summarize his most important teachings before, he, uh ..."

At that, it was Pete who let out a giant sob. Mr. Pilgrim put an arm around his son—just as Jesus began speaking.

> "If you love me, show it by doing what I've told you. I will talk to the Father, and he'll provide you another Friend so that you will always have someone with you. [At this point I joined in with all four Pilgrims and Jesna in a crying chorus.] This Friend is the Spirit of Truth. The godless world can't take him in because it doesn't have eyes to see him, doesn't know what to look for. But you know him already because he has been staying with you, and will even be *in* you!"[22]

"He's talking about himself, isn't he?" Priscilla whispered.

"That's right," Jesna said quietly. "He's the member of the Trinity that's been *with* them, in the flesh. And soon he'll be back as the Holy Spirit—to be in their flesh."

"Psst," Pete sprayed. "Is the Trinity three separate persons or just one?"

"Yes," Jesna said.

"Huh?"

> "I will not leave you orphaned," Jesus continued. "I'm coming back. In just a little while the world will no longer see me, but you're going to see me because I am alive and you're about to come alive. At that moment you will know absolutely that I'm in my Father, and you're in me, and I'm in you.
>
> "The person who knows my commandments and keeps them, that's who loves me. And the person who loves me will be loved by my Father, and I will love him and make myself plain to him."[23]

"What are the commandments?" Pete asked excitedly. "Tell 'em to me again, Jesna. And tell 'em plain, too. Because I'm going to start doing them—if that means Jesus will live inside me and be my friend."

"Love Jesus. And love every person you meet," Jesna said. "Those are *his* commandments."

"Yeah, I remember him saying those two a lot. But tell me again how I can do that second part—loving everybody in the world. It sounds impossible."

"It is completely impossible, Pete. I mean, impossible for a human to do. That's why you have to acknowledge that *you* can't, and then ask Jesus to live inside you and do it through you. He already knows how to love God and all the people in the world."

"How should I ask him?" Pete asked.

"You could say, 'Jesus, I really like you and respect you. Please come live in my heart and teach me how to love you fully and all the people you made, too.' Then, just move yourself out of the way and let him do it."

"That's where the Pharisees mess up, isn't it, Jesna?" Priscilla asked.

"Yes, Priscilla. They're trying to do the impossible, to obey God's commandments by their own efforts."

"And all that did was make them tired, grumpy, and tight-lipped. Huh, Jesna?"

"Yes, Pete. Trying to be God can be exhausting."

"Yeah," Pete said. "I think I would even need some help doing that."

"That 'helper' you need is who Jesus is talking about," Jesna said.

"I'm telling you these things while I'm still living with you. The Friend, the Holy Spirit whom the Father will send at my request, will make everything plain to you. He will remind you of all the things I have told you."[24]

"The Holy Spirit," Jesna said, "that's your friend and the only sword you can use to defeat the world."

FAMILY DISCUSSION

1. You may want to have a family discussion about how it is that Jesus is both one with his Father and the Holy Spirit, and yet separate. It may be helpful to envision a three-leaf clover, or water as liquid, ice, and steam.
2. How does it make you feel to know that you have Jesus as a counselor and friend—living inside you forever?
3. What are some things you need that friend to help you with tomorrow?

SCENE 192
THE GIFT OF PEACE[25]

Jesus continued instructing his dear friends. They sat motionless, mouths open, like hungry baby birds. I felt like we were all getting to listen to a private version of the sermon on the mountain—Jesus' final fireside chat. Being a dog, I was particularly impressed with how Jesus was saying he would be their faithful friend, forever. I've always thought humans would be a lot better off if they would be as loyal as us dogs.

"I'm leaving you well and whole. That's my parting gift to you. Peace. I don't leave you the way you're used to being left—feeling abandoned, bereft. So don't be upset. Don't be distraught.

"You've heard me tell you, 'I'm going away, and I'm coming back.' If you loved me, you would be glad that I'm on my way to the Father because the Father is the goal and purpose of my life.

"I've told you this ahead of time, before it happens, so that when it does happen, the confirmation will deepen your belief in me. I'll not be talking with you much more like this because the chief of this godless world is about to attack. But don't worry—he has nothing on me, no claim on me. But so the world might know how thoroughly I love the Father, I am carrying out my Father's instructions right down to the last detail."[26]

"Psst."

"Yes, Mr. Pilgrim?"

"Did Jesus just say that the devil is the chief of this world?"

"That's right," Jesna began. "The devil is often referred to by Jesus as the 'ruler,' or 'prince' of this world."

"But how can that be? God made the universe and everything in it. He's the ruler of the world."

"Oh no, Mr. Pilgrim. The 'world' has been temporarily taken over by another. You're right that God did make every atom in the universe. And he established the two rules necessary for enjoying life in his kingdom—being in love with him and his creation. But because of the gift of free will, we don't have to obey his rules. We can fall outside of his kingdom and live by our own rules."

"We're like Pinocchio after his strings got cut, huh, Jesna?"

"That's right, Pete. After his strings got cut and he got tricked into going into a faraway land."

"And made a donkey of himself," Pete said emphatically.

"And that's precisely what happened here on earth after Adam and Eve got tricked," she continued. "They left the garden and entered a dark and cold kingdom of selfishness and self-rule. That world has been under the thumb of God's archenemy—Satan. He's the ruler and prince here."

"That's why God sent his very own Son, right, Jesna?"

"That's right, Priscilla. Jesus has descended into the devil's domain to establish kingdom outposts—communities of people willing to surrender their self-rule and obey the rules of the King. Willing to leave their dark caves and step out into his holy light."

"Willing to listen to their hearts instead of their bellies?" Mr. Pilgrim asked as he gave Pete a playful eyebrow jiggle.

"Exactly right. But all this insubordination will make the world's ruler furious. That's what Jesus is warning his friends about. That's why he's comforting them by reminding them that he will not be leaving them alone. He himself, the King's

Son, will be returning to live in their hearts and help them battle the prince of this world."

"And since he's God," Priscilla began, "he already knows the future. He already knows who wins the battle down here."

"You're right, too, Priscilla. Having Jesus inside you and knowing that the prince of the world is already a defeated foe is precisely the *peace* that Jesus is leaving his friends."

FAMILY DISCUSSION

1. Let someone in the family retell the Pinocchio story, but with Geppetto using the methods that Jesus used to solve the dilemma. (Hint: He enters into "Candy Land" as a little boy himself.)

SCENE 193
JESUS THE TRUE VINE[27]

The night was clear and quiet. Every star in heaven was peeping out through a black quilt to see Jesus say goodbye to his friends. Each friend had become stone still, knowing that the snap of a twig could cost dearly, could cost the hearing of a word. Their only movement was an occasional tear-twinkle in a moist eye.

It was as if every atom in the universe knew what was happening and had stopped swirling. Their Creator had come to earth and poured his life into the hearts of a few very ordinary men. Now, on the eve of goodbye, it was time to say his most important words.

As we watched reverently, Jesus reached inside a cloth bag and pulled out a bunch of grapes. He studied the small cluster in his hand before speaking again.

> "I am the Vine, you are the branches. When you're joined with me and I with you, the relation [is] intimate and organic, the harvest is sure to be abundant. Separated, you can't produce a thing. Anyone who separates from me is deadwood, gathered up and thrown on the bonfire. But if you make yourselves at home with me and my words are at home in you, you can be sure that whatever you ask will be listened to and acted upon. This is how my Father shows who he is—when you produce grapes, when you mature as my disciples."[28]

"I don't quite get it," Priscilla whispered solemnly. "How can a person stay *in* Jesus, especially now that he's about to go away?"

"The same way he has stayed *in* his Father the last thirty-three years," Jesna spoke softly.

"Hmm?" Priscilla asked from deep in her throat.

"You know—how he almost always got up early in the morning and went off to a quiet place to pray, to be with his Dad. And how he studied the Scriptures until he had learned most by heart."

"Psst. Jesna. It's a little easier for him to memorize the Bible. He wrote it."

"Yes, Pete, you're right. But it was his love for his Father and for his words that caused him to spend so much time *in* both."

Pete looked a little puzzled and Jesna continued. "Imagine a grapevine planted next to a beautiful stream."

Pete immediately closed his eyes to get a better view of what Jesna was saying.

"The vine isn't in the middle of the flowing water. It's on a bank close by. Now picture that the vine begins to sink its roots deep into the ground, so deep that they begin to sip from the wet ground beside and underneath the stream. What happens then?"

"The vine gets to guzzle from the stream."

"Yes, Pete. The grapevine drinks from the stream, takes water into its roots and branches and out into its fruit. It flourishes by doing that—even if the rains stop for a while. It is *in* the stream and life from the stream is in it."

"Is that why Jesus has spent so much time alone with God?"

"Yes, Priscilla. And he wants his disciples to realize that they can do the same thing. When someone begins to practice the Christian disciplines of listening-prayer, Scripture reading, worship, fasting, and God-inspired giving, they are *in* God and drinking from his River of Life, his Spirit. And when they don't ..."

"They become like my teacher, ole Mrs.—"

"Pete!" Mrs. Pilgrim whisper-shouted.

"Well, even Dad said she was a mean ole dried-up prune...."

"Pete!" Mr. Pilgrim shouted.

"And when they (or we) don't stay plugged *into* God's love, it's impossible to produce fruit—God-grapes to give others who are hungry. Isn't that what you were trying to say, Pete?"

"I couldn't have said it better, Jesna."

"So," Priscilla said, "Jesus wants us to live in a way that keeps us connected to him and his Father."

"Yes, Priscilla," Jesna said. "So that divine life and spirit begin to flow into you. And that's the most important thing he can leave with his friends."

"And," Priscilla interrupted, "it's important

that they get it. After all, in just a few days, it will be their job to begin planting kingdom vineyards in the devil's backyard."

"They sure had better stay close to the water supply, then," Pete offered, "or they could end up like ole Mrs.—"

Clamp! went three Pilgrim hands across Pete's mouth.

FAMILY DISCUSSION

1. What does it mean for you to be *in* Christ, as a branch is *in* a vine?
2. What is some of the fruit you have grown during times you were *in* Jesus?
3. What are your biggest obstacles to staying *grafted* into Jesus?

SCENE 194

ABIDE IN MY LOVE[29]

Jesus gently laid the small bunch of grapes inside a receptive fold on the outside of the cloth bag that had been their home. He continued talking to his dear friends—whom he had taken out from the world—about the fruit that would soon grow from their branches if they stayed connected to him, the Vine.

> "I've loved you the way my Father has loved me. Make yourselves at home in my love. If you keep my commands, you'll remain intimately at home in my love. That's what I've done—kept my Father's commands and made myself at home in his love.
>
> "I've told you these things for a purpose: that my joy might be your joy, and your joy wholly mature. This is my command: Love one another the way I loved you. This is the very best way to love. Put your life on the line for your friends. You are my friends when you do the things I com-

mand you. I'm no longer calling you servants because servants don't understand what their master is thinking and planning. No, I've named you friends because I've let you in on everything I've heard from the Father.

"You didn't choose me, remember; I chose you, and put you in the world to bear fruit, fruit that won't spoil. As fruit bearers, whatever you ask the Father in relation to me, he gives you.

"But remember the root command: Love one another."[30]

Jesus paused, allowing time for his words to soak into the fertile hearts of his friends.

But Pete had never been one to put up with much "soaking" time. A few nanoseconds into the lull, he asked Jesna, "Is Jesus saying that I'm his friend, too? 'Cause I want to be his friend more than anything!"

"You bet, Pete. Anyone who chooses to stay close to the King—lives *in* him and obeys his rules—becomes his friend."

"Even if they've been a serf?"

"Especially if they've been a serf, Pete."

"Well, what kind of fruit will I be growing if I'm one of his friend-branches?"

"Love, Pete. Love and peace and joy are the three main types of fruit that Jesus' friends grow out of their hearts."

"I think I've heard him say some of these things before," Priscilla inserted. "Is Jesus saying anything new tonight, Jesna?"

"Oh no, Priscilla. He's just summarizing what he's said before."

"Well, summarize it for me again, Jesna," Pete requested. "I like summaries. They don't take up as much room in my brain."

"You do it, Pete. It's already in your brain. You tell me what things you've heard Jesus say most often."

"It seems like three things have come up an awful lot," Pete began. "Jesus talked about the kingdom almost every day. And he talked about how we should stick close to God and do what he says…."

"Yes, Pete, go on," Jesna encouraged.

"And he got yelled at by the Pharisees a whole bunch. I think those are the three main things that kept coming up."

"Pete, I think you are a great summarizer. Jesus came to earth to do one thing—to replant the Garden of Eden—he calls it 'the kingdom of heaven'—in people's hearts.

"But to keep their soul-gardens growing and producing fruit, people need to know another thing—that they must stay close to their Maker and drink from his spirit-streams of life. Whoever keeps their hearts irrigated by God's love will grow mounds of fruit—love, peace, and joy—and will become his friends."

"So, Jesna, why did Jesus have such a hard time getting along with the Pharisees?" Pete asked.

"Because when he came they were doing all the gardening work on their own," Jesna answered. "They had no need for a gardener, and saw no necessity to move closer to the holy stream."

"And their branches," Mrs. Pilgrim inserted, "were barren of God-fruit."

"Yeah," Pete said. "They didn't even know they were growing persimmons instead of the good stuff."

"And," Priscilla added, "they've been growing anger, competition, and sternness, instead of love, peace, and joy."

"That's right," Jesna said. "Most Pharisees keep their hearts far from God's River of Life. So they have to try to water their gardens with the sweat of their brow."

"Pretty difficult to grow joy out of a hard, dry heart, with only forehead sweat for water, huh, Jesna?"

"Yes, Pete. That would be impossible. And that's exactly what Jesus wants his dear friends to remember. He's the vine and they're the branches."

"And," Pete blurted out, "to grow holy fruit you'll be needin' to stay close to the holy water."

FAMILY DISCUSSION

1. Where do you feel most at home—in God's kingdom—or in the world?
2. To feel at home in God's kingdom is to feel like being in love. Since the best way to keep loving feelings in your heart is to keep giving love away, what are some ways you can give love to your family members tomorrow?

SCENE 195
THE WORLD'S HATRED[31]

Night had now completely fallen. In the distance, other Passover pilgrims were moving around their campsites on the Mount of Olives—preparing for lights out. But the gravity of being with Jesus made it seem as if those surrounding us were in a wholly different world. Their muffled noises rarely penetrated our quiet—and I have doggy ears.

Jesus reached over and plucked a grape from the bunch he had set down earlier. He studied the small red ball for a few seconds.

"Isn't it neat how God made grapes in their own individually wrapped containers?" Pete observed. When no one responded he continued, "Maybe that's where M&M's got the idea for stuff not melting in your hands."

That brought the groans he was gunning for.

Then without saying a word, Jesus crushed the grape between his fingers. He looked very sad as the juice ran down his hand, and he began to speak again.

> "If you find the godless world is hating you, remember it got its start hating me. If you lived on the world's terms, the world would love you as one of its own. But since I picked you to live on God's terms and no longer on the world's terms, the world is going to hate you."

"And try to crush your spirit?" Pete asked.

> "When that happens, remember this: Servants don't get better treatment than their masters. If they beat on me, they will certainly beat on you. If they did what I told them, they will do what you tell them.
>
> "They are going to do all these things to you because of the way they treated me, because they don't know the One who sent me. If I hadn't come and told them all this in plain language, it wouldn't be so bad. As it is, they have no excuse. Hate me, hate my Father—it's all the same. If I hadn't done what I have done among them, works no one has *ever* done, they wouldn't be to blame. But they saw the God-signs and hated anyway, both me and my Father. Interesting—they have verified the truth of their own Scriptures where it is written, 'They hated me for no good reason.'"[32]

"Jesus?"

"Yes, Priscilla."

"What's the difference between living on the world's terms and living on God's terms?"

"Umpfft!" Pete grunted. "You mean you've been following Jesus around for thirty-three Bible years and you don't know that? What kind of a genius are you, anyway?"

"I mean *exactly* what is the difference, Pete? I want her to tell me in simple terms—like what even you could understand."

"Oh, that's different.... Wait a minute!"

"Children!" Mrs. Pilgrim scolded. "I want to hear Jesna's answer."

"So do I," said Mr. Pilgrim. "I make my living out there in the world. I have to deal with its 'terms' every day."

"I don't think I have an opinion that's worth all that buildup," Jesna began. "But here's what I think.

"The world is the realm of earth-life that is ruled over by the prince of lies. It's visible and it appears (to earth dwellers) to be right side up. The kingdom, to those on the earth, is invisible and upside down. It's ruled over by God. And it exists wherever people are abiding in their heavenly Father and obeying his rules.

"To live your life on the world's terms means that your daily existence is characterized by competition, comparisons, fear, anger, despair, and self-rule. Power and money determine who serves and who is served. Happiness is short-lived and generally connected to short-term gains of money or power.

"To live life on God's terms means that your life is painted from a totally different palette. Cooperation, humility, peace, love, and joy color your life. Power and money are viewed with indifference because being a subject of the King brings far more rewards than one could ever seize or buy.

"But living on God's terms makes you a threat to the

world. You become a spirit-set-free, no longer susceptible to being controlled by the world's ways of determining who is important and who is not."

"So is that why the people with power in the world have come to hate Jesus so much with no good reason?" Pete asked. "Because he won't play the game by their rules?"

"Yes, Pete. Living in the kingdom is a whole new game, with a totally different set of rules."

Pete studied our campfire-dotted surroundings with a thoughtful gaze. "Do you think some of these people will learn to live their lives on God's terms?" he asked.

"With Jesus having so many friends like you, Pete, I think the prince of this world is in serious trouble."

FAMILY DISCUSSION

1. Have you ever been rejected because you did something Jesus' way instead of the world's way?
2. Tell everyone about it and what you learned from the experience.
3. If you decide that tomorrow you will wake up and live every minute of the day by God's rules instead of the world's, what changes will that make in how you live the day?

SCENE 196

THE WITNESS OF THE PARACLETE[33]

I walked over to where Jesus was sitting and tried to lick the juice from his fingers. I wasn't thirsty, but somehow it made me feel real sad to see it there. Being a hologram, however, I wasn't able to get it off. Jesus gave me a pat on the head for my effort and that set my tail to wagging. It took care of those sad feelings, too.

When I walked back to Pete's side he gave me a scratch behind the ear and said, "Good dog." My tail shifted into second gear.

I could tell, though, when I surveyed the faces of the disciples that they weren't in a tail-wagging mood. Most looked very sad. A few looked a little scared. And one looked mad as a wet cat. Maybe that's why Jesus began talking again—to give them a pat on the head.

> "When the Friend I plan to send you from the Father comes—the Spirit of Truth issuing from the Father—he will confirm everything about me. You, too, from your side must give your confirming evidence, since you are in this with me from the start."[34]

I glanced up at Pete. From the look on his face I could tell he was sucking in air to blow out a question. And judging from the size of the inhale, it stood to be a big one.

"Jesna?"

"Yes, Pete."

"Who all is living back where Jesus is from?"

"In Nazareth?"

"No, up in heaven."

"Oh, I was afraid that was what you meant," Jesna said. "There's his Father and all the angels—"

"So," Pete interrupted, "is the friend Jesus mentioned an angel?"

"Oh no! The Friend is the Holy Spirit of God."

"So it's God that's coming back?"

"Yes, as the Holy Spirit."

"What's the difference?" Pete asked. "You didn't explain

about the Trinity when I asked before. So this time take your time. And while you're 'splainin', tell me how it is that Jesus, who is standing right over there, is also God—who's up in heaven."

"Oh my," Jesna replied, "that's a big question."

I, of course, already knew a big question was coming. I'd seen Pete suck in half the air on the Mount of Olives before asking it.

"Well," Jesna began, "*you* are created in the image of God. And even though there's only one of you, you have three parts."

"My belly, my head, and, uh, what else?"

"No. I'm referring to the fact that you have a mind, a body, and a spirit."

"Oh. I see. Sort of."

"God," Jesna continued, "is also *one* and *three*. In a way, God, Jesus, and the Holy Spirit—who are only one being—are like a single person, existing as mind, body, and spirit.

"And now that God will soon be removing from human sight one aspect of himself—as expressed through Jesus—he will be sending another: a live-in, twenty-four-hour-a-day Friend."

"I still don't quite get it," Pete announced. "Why doesn't he just stay, if he's going to be coming right back?"

"Pete, I know this is hard to grasp, but God is omnipresent."

"Huh?"

"He is everywhere all at the same time. God, Jesus, and the Holy Spirit are all one being who has always been, always will be, and exists in every square inch of the universe, all at the same time.

"He (God) chose to break into this world in human form

(Jesus) so that people could understand him better, understand how much he loves them and misses them."

"And maybe so he could reach out and give them a hug?" Pete asked.

"Yes, Pete. And the Friend who will come (actually, he's always been here, too) will be God in a different form—a form capable of living on the inside of a person. A form capable of whispering to humans down deep in their hearts."

"To give their insides a hug?"

"You could say that, Pete."

"I think I get it," Priscilla announced. "While God is just one person ... uh, being ... he sent an aspect of himself (Jesus) who could talk with us face-to-face. And he'll make another aspect of himself known to us who can live on our insides and talk to us spirit-to-spirit."

"That's it, too!" Jesna said.

While Mr. and Mrs. Pilgrim were slowly nodding their understanding, I was left scratching my own head. I wasn't sure I got all of that. But I guess I'll never understand why anyone would pet a cat, either. Some things are just beyond reason.

Pete had bent down for a closer inspection of the ground. When he straightened up he was holding a three-leaf clover. "I think I get it, too," he announced.

FAMILY DISCUSSION

1. What are some advantages of having a twenty-four-hour-a-day counselor living inside your heart?
2. Sometimes people feel overwhelmed because they only ask their holy Friend for advice after things have piled up in their life. What are some ways that you can remind yourself to live in a spirit of prayer—all the time? (Hint: Some people find it helpful to set their watches to alarm every sixty minutes—as

a reminder to pray for guidance. Some have learned to whisper a prayer for God's help before beginning any new task; and some even say "thanks" when they are finished.)

SCENE 197
ON PERSECUTIONS[35]

Noise from the surrounding campsites was becoming less frequent. Most of the sharp sounds had disappeared, replaced by the funny groans and tones humans make when they sleep.

Lights were also dimming. Most of the flames that had danced in the air above a hundred distant campfires had gone inside their wooden houses for the night. They glowed quietly from in between brown and ember-white walls, almost asleep themselves.

Jerusalem itself was beginning to dim as torch after torch was extinguished. The city walls and buildings were becoming less golden and more gray-brown.

My attention was called back to Jesus. He had drawn in a slow, deep breath. From the long sigh that followed, it was obvious that he was about to say more—and that it would be hard to say. All of us knew his earth-light was about to go out as well.

"I've told you these things to prepare you for rough times ahead. They are going to throw you out of the meeting places. There will even come a time when anyone who kills you will think he's doing God a favor. They will do these things because they never really understood the Father. I've told you these things so that when the time comes and they start in on you, you'll be well-warned and ready for them."[36]

"That is almost inconceivable," Mr. Pilgrim said.

"What's that, Dad?" Priscilla asked.

"For anyone to kill one of Jesus' closest friends as if that was doing God a favor. How can that be?"

"Maybe they don't spend much time hanging out with God," Pete mused. "'Cause if they did they'd know that Jesus was his boy—and they'd know who Jesus' friends are, too."

As Mr. Pilgrim was looking at his son and nodding understanding, Priscilla spoke up.

"I think Pete is right, Dad. Jesus said the people who would do that never really understood his Father. And I think that the only way to understand somebody is to spend time with him. What do you think, Jesna?"

"I think your Father has two spiritually bright children. Recognizing God as a *real* Father who wants to spend lots of time hanging out with his children is the first step toward life in his kingdom."

"What are the next steps?" Priscilla asked.

"To ask him to come live in your heart and then to ask him to help you obey his rules—the rules of kingdom life. And," Jesna said, anticipating Pete's question, "those rules are simple—you've heard Jesus say them over and over. Stay in love with God and share that love with all his other children."

"So," Pete began, "anybody who will take the time to sit around a campfire and talk to God—*and really get to know him*—would never do something stupid, like hurting one of his friends."

"That's right, Pete. If you'll prepare a seat for God and keep the fire tended, you'll never be in the dark. And you'll never do anything so stupid as what you are about to see."

FAMILY DISCUSSION

1. How do you think Jesus' friends will feel when Jesus' enemies start mistreating them?
2. If you were his friend, what would you do to hold on to your faith in Jesus?

SCENE 198

THE WORK OF THE PARACLETE[37]

Even though Jesus had just told his friends that they would be rejected—kicked out of synagogues—and that some might even be killed, a quick study of their eyes revealed more sadness than fear. Even Pete's eyes were watery sad, instead of fiery mad. I think Jesus saw it, too.

"I didn't tell you this earlier because I was with you every day. But now I am on my way to the One who sent me. Not one of you has asked, 'Where are you going?' Instead, the longer I've talked, the sadder you've become. So let me say it again, this truth: It's better for you that I leave. If I don't leave, the Friend won't come. But if I go, I'll send him to you.

"When he comes, he'll expose the error of the godless world's view of sin, righteousness, and judgment: He'll show them that their refusal to believe in me is their basic sin; that righteousness comes from above, where I am with the Father, out of their sight and control; that judgment takes place as the ruler of this godless world is brought to trial and convicted.

"I still have many things to tell you, but you can't handle them now. But when the Friend comes, the Spirit of the

Truth, he will take you by the hand and guide you into all the truth there is. He won't draw attention to himself, but will make sense out of what is about to happen and, indeed, out of all that I have done and said. He will honor me; he will take from me and deliver it to you. Everything the Father has is also mine. That is why I've said, 'He takes from me and delivers to you.'

"In a day or so you're not going to see me, but then in another day or so you will see me."[38]

Question marks had formed in the wet eyes of most of the disciples. As they began to murmur to one another about what Jesus meant, it was obvious that Jesus would have more 'splainin' to do.

But before their questions were turned into words, Priscilla fired off the first round.

"Jesna, what is the Truth that Jesus keeps talking about? And what is the Lie that the ruler of this world—the devil—keeps spreading around?"

"The Truth," Jesna began, "is very simple. God, who exists in three forms, is your *real* Father. He wants to live with you, his child, and he wants to walk and talk with you—as he did with his kids in the Garden of Eden.

"Ever since Adam and Eve left home, he's sent prophets, and now his very own Son to say, 'Come back. Come back home and live in the garden—the kingdom of heaven.'

"And the Truth is, to stay there, all you have to do is obey his rules and eat from the Tree of Life—that is to say, stay connected to him like branches into a vine. Draw your life from God."

"And the Lie is?" Priscilla asked.

"The Lie is that God is not your *real* Father and that he does not have your best interests at heart. The Lie says you are better off by eating from a different tree, a tree that would make you like God—in control of your life, and independent from him."

"So," Pete said, "the Truth is, God should be running your life, and the Lie is that you could do a better job of it by yourself."

"You got it, Little Theologian," Jesna said. "And I hope you get this, too. The worst lie of all is that you can have the best of both worlds. That's what all imitation religions offer. They provide the false sense that you can have your bags packed for glory and stored in the trunk while never turning the steering wheel over to God."

FAMILY DISCUSSION

1. What does it feel like when you allow God to sit behind the steering wheel of your life?
2. Since you did this—turned your life over to God—have you ever been tempted to be a back-seat driver? Have you ever crawled back into the front seat and taken control of the wheel?
3. How do you think this "driving" metaphor relates to eating from the two different trees in the Garden of Eden?

SCENE 199
SORROW TURNED TO JOY[39]

I could see a storm of mixed emotions blowing across the eyes of his friends. I'm sure Jesus saw it, too. He watched as the turbulence turned into a small tempest of questions.

"What's he talking about?" one asked.

"Yeah. What does he mean, 'In a day or so you're not going to see me, but then in another day or so you will see me'?"

"I don't know," whispered a third. "I don't even know what Jesus meant when he said he's 'on the way to the Father.' It could be Joseph he's talking about … or it could be he's going to see God."

"And what is this 'day or so'?" asked a fourth—to no one in particular. "I don't think any of us understand what he is telling us."

Jesus seemed to know his friends were dying to ask him what he meant but were too embarrassed to direct their questions to him. He smiled and said,

> "Are you trying to figure out among yourselves what I meant when I said, 'In a day or so you're not going to see me, but then in another day or so you will see me'?"

"I think I get it," Pete whispered to Jesna. "But I guess you could say that I'm two thousand years older than any of these guys."

Jesus continued:

> "Fix this firmly in your minds: You're going to be in deep mourning while the godless world throws a party. You'll be sad, very sad, but your sadness will develop into gladness.
>
> "When a woman gives birth, she has a hard time, there's no getting around it. But when the baby is born, there is joy in the birth. This new life in the world wipes out memory of the pain. The sadness you have right now is similar to that pain, but the coming joy is also similar. When I see you again, you'll be full of joy, and it will be a joy no one can rob from you. You'll no longer be so full of questions."[40]

"Yep," Pete crowed. "I definitely got it."

"Well, since you won't give us any peace until you blurt it out, let's hear what you think you got, little brother."

Pete leaned in and began to whisper, "Jesus is going to have to die real soon. Right?"

We all nodded a sad "yes."

"After he dies we all know that he goes away to be with his Father in heaven. But you see, those disciples don't understand that yet. They're still writing all those Sunday school books we've already read. And they haven't yet written the chapter Jesus is talking about.

"When he goes away they're going to be real sad. They'll probably feel even worse than if their dog died."

I had to admit that Pete had a way with words.

"And," Pete continued, "I guess it'll hurt them like it hurts a woman when she has a baby. Although I don't know a lot about that part myself, but I heard Mom say it hurt worse than having a cantaloupe come out your nose.

"And to make it even worse, while they're in pain and crying, the world will be throwing a party. The religious leaders that hate Jesus don't know nothin' about birthin' no spiritual babies. They'll think all the pain just means that their biggest enemy is dead and gone.

"But in a few days things will be turned upside down. Jesus will come back to earth, come back to life, BOOM! just like that. Then it will be his friends throwing the party. Then they'll know that Jesus is exactly who he's been saying he is—God's own Son.

"They'll be as happy as new dads in delivery rooms. Shoot, they'll be as happy as parents at a funeral who just saw their child jump up out of the casket and say, 'Let's go to the park!' They'll be happy as both those things—all rolled into one big joy-feeling. When that happens their eyes will dry up. They'll have to be careful not to explode."

"Pete?"

"Yes, Mom?"

"I think you're exactly right about what Jesus is trying to tell them."

"Yes," Jesna said. "And you're even right about the explosion, Pete. It'll be sad for Jesus' friends for a while. But they'll blow up into a billion-member church—even bigger. And that's a whole lot of new births to be excited about."

I think a few of the disciples got what Jesus was saying, too. But for now, the clouds in their eyes were beginning to rain.

FAMILY DISCUSSION

1. If you have ever had a time where a sadness was turned into joy, tell each other about it. A joy shared is doubled.
2. If your sadness is still a sadness for you, tell that, too. A sadness shared is often cut in half.

SCENE 200
PRAYER IN THE NAME OF JESUS[41]

Seeing that his friends were still full of questions, Jesus became very direct.

> "This is what I want you to do: Ask the Father for whatever is in keeping with the things I've revealed to you. Ask in my name, according to my will, and he'll most certainly give it to you. Your joy will be a river overflowing its banks!
>
> "I've used figures of speech in telling you these things. Soon I'll drop the figures and tell you about the Father in

plain language. Then you can make your requests directly to him in relation to this life I've revealed to you. I won't continue making requests of the Father on your behalf. I won't need to. Because you've gone out on a limb, committed yourselves to love and trust in me, believing I came directly from the Father, the Father loves you directly. First, I left the Father and arrived in the world; now I leave the world and travel to the Father."[42]

"So," Priscilla began, "that's something I've always wondered about. When we pray, are we supposed to be talking to God or to Jesus?"

"Yeah," Pete chimed in. "After having spent the last thirty-three years with Jesus, it seems more natural now to talk to him when I pray. But I don't want to offend his Dad or anything."

Jesna was smiling one of her sly smiles, the kind she smiles just before a good story.

"I think the *what* and *where* are more important than the *to whom*," she began.

"What?" asked all four Pilgrims.

"That's right," Jesna continued with a giggle. "*What*. But even though you've got it, a story might be in order."

"Oh boy!" Pete said. "I love your stories. And," he continued with one arched eyebrow, "I'm not sure I got what you're saying yet, either."

The four Pilgrims quickly joined with Pete in making a circle around their little tour guide. I squeezed in between the youngest two. It was their custom to scratch my head while listening. I didn't want to disappoint them.

"Once upon a time ..." Jesna began.

"I love stories that start with that."

"Shhhh, Pete!"

"… there was a large house that sat in the middle of a huge fenced-in estate."

"Was it a gingerbread house?" Pete asked.

"No," Jesna said, "just a plain ole stone mansion with a wraparound porch."

"Oh well, sounds pretty nice, even if you can't eat it."

"The front gate to the manor was always left wide open. And in the front yard the owner had planted beautiful gardens and built a large playground. The combination of an open gate and a lovely place to play was more than some kids in the neighborhood could resist."

"I can sure understand that," Pete quipped before his sister's hand came to rest on his mouth.

"Sometimes," Jesna continued, "a few brave children would sneak in through the open gate and climb on the shiny metal and painted-wood playground equipment. But being afraid of the owner, they would only stay a short time before scurrying off. And with the children thinking only of themselves—and hoping to grab as much fun as possible in a short time—they found the playground equipment was very hard to operate.

"One child discovered that the seesaw was only good for one bone-jarring *see*—from sky to ground. Another child could barely set the heavy swing in motion—even with lots of leg-pumping. And one by one the children tried to get the tilt-a-whirl to spin, but no one could get the sluggish ride to budge.

"Then one day a youngster emerged from the front door of the mansion. He began to play in the gardens. Children from the neighborhood stuck their heads through the wrought-iron fence to watch.

"When he walked over to the playground, the onlookers' hearts began to beat with excitement. With a hand on the seesaw he motioned for the watching children to join him. They raced through the open gate and began to assault the playground in their usual self-centered manner.

"'No! No!' the house-dweller laughed. 'That's not how it works. Slow down. Take your time. Better yet, watch me.'

"Then he showed them how children playing together can set seesaws in perpetual motion, cause swings to tickle stomachs, and tilt-a-whirls to tilt and whirl. He showed them how love, cooperation, and thinking of another's joy can double your own.

"After a day of joyous fun and feasting from a bottomless picnic basket, the child who had taught the others how to play together said that he must go back inside—to be with his father. He thanked them for becoming his friends. He told them that they no longer needed to sneak around the estate in fear. It was theirs to enjoy.

"He also told them something else."

"What! What!" Pete asked. "Was there a chocolate fountain in the backyard?"

"He told them his father loved them, that he considered them to be his very own children, too.

"'When you come back to play,' he said to his open-mouthed friends, 'come right up to the front door and ring the bell. When my father, that is, *your* father, comes to the door, tell him that you have become my friends. Then ask him for anything that is in keeping with what I have showed you—putting others' pleasure before your own—and he'll give it to you.'"

"So," Jesna said, ending her story. "Now do you understand what Jesus is saying?"

"If the front gate is open, jump on the seesaw?" Pete asked.

"Nope," Jesna said.

"I think I do," Mrs. Pilgrim said. "I think he is saying that it is very important that *what* you ask be in keeping with his teachings about love and sharing."

"Yes," Priscilla said. "God probably isn't going to be very happy if you ask him to send everybody else home so you can swing by yourself."

Mrs. Pilgrim gave her daughter a nod and continued. "And *where* you ask should be from the center of his will—standing on the front porch, asking as a friend of Jesus."

"That's right," Jesna said with a proud smile. "And while it is very proper to show God the respect of directing our requests to him—in the name of his Son—it is very heartwarming to know that God, Jesus, and his Holy Spirit are one. It was also God who was playing with those children. It is also God who is over there," Jesna said as she pointed to Jesus with her forehead, "talking with his friends."

FAMILY DISCUSSION

1. When you pray, is it your custom to address God, the Father, or Jesus?
2. Have you done what Jesus was so proud of his disciples for doing—going "out on a limb" to believe that Jesus came directly from the Father and that the Father loves you directly?

SCENE 201

PREDICTION OF THE DISCIPLES' FLIGHT[43]

Most of the campers on the Mount of Olives were fast asleep. Torches had been extinguished and campfires had changed from orange flames to white coals. The night was clear. Only an occasional wisp of cloud blocked the moonlight from shining on the disciples' faces.

Our attention was called away from discussing Jesna's story. The disciples were talking to Jesus—with considerable energy.

"Yes," one said, "you're giving it to us straight, in plain talk."

"Now," began another, "we know that you know everything. Everything comes together in you."

This brought a smile (a relieved smile) to Jesus' face. His smile broadened when another said, "You won't be bothered by all our questions anymore. You've convinced us. You came from God."

Jesus' smile was a short-lived comet. He looked into the embers of the fire for several seconds. His smile went out.

"Psst," Pete sprayed. "What's he staring at? It looks like he's looking into a crystal ball."

"That's not it, Pete," Jesna whispered. "But he *is* feeling what the future holds."

Jesus broke eye contact with the coals and said to his friends,

> "Do you finally believe? In fact, you're about to make a run for it—saving your own skins and abandoning me. But I'm not abandoned. The Father is with me. I've told you all this so that trusting me, you will be unshakable and assured, deeply at peace. In this godless world you will continue to experience difficulties. But take heart! I've conquered the world."[44]

A long silence followed. Somewhere in the midst of it Jesus closed his eyes. His lips began to move in silent prayer. His eyelashes became dams—holding back the raging flood of emotion.

"Let's get closer to Jesus," Pete said. "I want to hear what he's praying."

"Oh, you'll be able to hear very soon, Pete," Jesna answered as she put a restraining hand on Pete's arm. "In just a few moments Jesus will open his mouth and pray one of the most famous prayers in all of Scripture. It will become known as 'The High Priestly Prayer of Jesus.' It's a special prayer for his followers."

"Well, while we're waiting for that, maybe you could whisper to me about how Jesus conquers the world. I mean, I haven't seen any planes, or tanks, or mushroom clouds."

"No, you haven't, Pete," Jesna said. "And you won't during Jesus' time here on earth. The world that Jesus has been in and *is* conquering is the invisible realm of the devil. And it's being conquered by living out a simple principle."

"What is it?" Priscilla asked.

"Loving God. Trusting that he loves you. And being willing to obey him—even if it means death. Jesus is defeating Satan with four words: *Love,* and *obedience unto death.*"

FAMILY DISCUSSION

1. How do you think the disciples felt when Jesus told them that they would soon deny knowing him—to "save their skins"?
2. How do you suppose Jesus would feel if you acted in a way that put distance between the two of you?
3. Are there any ways that you deny knowing Jesus?

SCENE 202
JESUS' HIGH PRIESTLY PRAYER—PART I[45]

Jesus' eyelashes did not work well as dams. Tears overflowed and began to make creek beds down his cheeks. He raised his face to heaven, his countenance aglow with moonlight.

After a few moments, a deeply peaceful expression spread across the terrain of his shining face. It was as if he had heard some unspoken communication—missed by everyone else. With this visible change of emotion, he began to pray—for all to hear—the second most famous prayer recorded in Scripture.

"Father, it's time.
Display the bright splendor of your Son
So the Son in turn may show your bright splendor.
You put him in charge of everything human
So he might give real and eternal life to all in his charge.
And this is the real and eternal life:
That they know you,
The one and only true God,
And Jesus Christ, whom you sent.
I glorified you on earth
By completing down to the last detail
What you assigned me to do.
And now, Father, glorify me with your very own splendor,
The very splendor I had in your presence
Before there was a world.

"I spelled out your character in detail
To the men and women you gave me.
They were yours in the first place;
They you gave them to me,

And they have now done what you said.
They know now, beyond the shadow of a doubt,
That everything you gave me is firsthand from you,
For the message you gave me, I gave them;
And they took it, and were convinced
That I came from you.
They believed that you sent me.
I pray for them.
I'm not praying for the God-rejecting world
But for those you gave me,
For they are yours by right.
Everything mine is yours, and yours mine,
And my life is on display in them.
For I'm no longer going to be visible in the world;
They'll continue in the world
While I return to you.
Holy Father, guard them as they pursue this life
That you conferred as a gift through me,
So they can be one heart and mind
As we are one heart and mind.
As long as I was with them, I guarded them
In pursuit of the life you gave through me;
I even posted a night watch.
And not one of them got away,
Except the rebel bent on destruction
(the exception that proved the rule of Scripture).

"Now I'm returning to you.
I'm saying these things in the world's hearing
So my people can experience
My joy completed in them."[46]

FAMILY DISCUSSION

1. Perhaps now (right in the middle of Jesus' special prayer for his followers) would be a good time for you to hold hands as a family and ask God to seal in your hearts everything you have learned about the life and character of Jesus. Then pray that his life will be on display in all you say and do.

SCENE 203
JESUS' HIGH PRIESTLY PRAYER—PART II[47]

The eleven disciples and four Pilgrims settled into a sacred hush as Jesus continued asking his Father to take care of them—after his return to heaven.

"I gave them your word;
The godless world hated them because of it,
Because they didn't join the world's ways,
Just as I didn't join the world's ways.
I'm not asking that you take them out of the world
But that you guard them from the Evil One.
They are no more defined by the world
Than I am defined by the world.
Make them holy—consecrated—with the truth;
Your word is consecrating truth.
In the same way that you gave me a mission in the world,
I give them a mission in the world.
I'm consecrating myself for their sakes
So they'll be truth-consecrated in their mission.

"I'm praying not only for them
But also for those who will believe in me
Because of them and their witness about me.

The goal is for all, them to become one heart and mind—
Just as you, Father, are in me and I in you,
So they might be one heart and mind with us.
Then the world might believe that you, in fact, sent me.
The same glory you gave me, I gave them,
So they'll be as unified and together as we are—
I in them and you in me.
Then they'll be mature in this oneness,
And give the godless world evidence
That you've sent me and loved them
In the same way you've loved me.

"Father, I want those you gave me
To be with me, right where I am,
So they can see my glory, the splendor you gave me,
Having loved me
Long before there ever was a world.
Righteous Father, the world has never known you,
But I have known you, and these disciples know
That you sent me on this mission.
I have made your very being known to them—
Who you are and what you do—
And continue to make it known,
So that your love for me
Might be in them
Exactly as I am in them."[48]

FAMILY PRAYER

1. Let someone reread the above prayer while everyone else sits with their eyes closed. Then spend several minutes of silent prayer and listening before God—experiencing the love of God that is in you, his friend.

SCENE 204
GETHSEMANE[49]

Jesus finished his conversation with his heavenly Father.

He looked at his disciples. Their faces were barely visible in the darkness, their expressions reflecting awe.

And why not? They had heard their friend talking to the Creator of life. Jesus had called him "Father"—and had asked that he take care of his friends.

Jesus arose from his cross-legged position and gestured for his disciples to follow. After a few bone-popping stretches, we were at their heels.

Jesus was leading the way down a gentle slope. We followed with cautious feet. Fortunately, a well-worn path stretched out before us; unfortunately, it was rutted by erosion.

"He's going to cross over the brook Kidron," Jesna said. "We'll be fording at a place where there is a beautiful garden on the other side."

True to Jesna's perfect-tour-guide record, a rippling brook soon came into view.

Jesus and the disciples began to take off their sandals. Soon they were lifting their robes and wading into the shallow water. Pete took the opportunity to race out ahead, into the middle of the stream.

"Look at this, Jesus!" he shouted gleefully, tossing double-handed cups of water into the night air. Fat waterdrops became translucent in the moonlight and rained on Pete's head.

Jesus greeted Pete with a forced smile but continued through the water to the garden—the Garden of Gethsemane—with a determined look. Seeing Pete's falling droplets (but not Pete), the disciples must have thought a huge school of salmon was making its way upstream.

"Good try, little brother," Priscilla said. "But I guess Jesus has too much on his mind tonight for much joking around."

Jesna was bringing up the rear. She was wearing a gloomy face. When she stepped up onto the bank, she said softly, "You may be interested in knowing something about this brook—Kidron. It feeds the Pool of Siloam, inside the city of Jerusalem."

"I remember the Pool of Siloam," Priscilla said. "It's the most important water supply for Jerusalem."

"That's right," Jesna said. "It's the lifeline to the Holy City—as Jesus should be."

After crossing the brook, Jesus entered the garden. He walked a few paces across soft grass, then told the disciples, "Stay here while I go over there and pray."

He motioned for Peter, James, and John to go with him. The four slowly began walking as a group. We followed, too. It was plain to see that with each step Jesus took he seemed a little more troubled and weighed down. It was as if gravity was pulling him hellward with heavy chains.

After they had separated themselves from the others by

about ten city lawns, Jesus stopped. Turning to face his three special friends, he said,

> "This sorrow is crushing my life out. Stay here and keep vigil with me."[50]

The three disciples gave him assuring looks.

Going ahead a little farther, Jesus fell on his face and began to pray. His whole body shook with prayer, as if an earthquake were "richtering" inside.

He prayed that way for a long time. Pete and Priscilla crept over and sat by his side. Close by his side. They didn't disturb him. They just sat close and let their hearts break with his pain.

Then after about an hour, Jesus suddenly cried a pleading prayer from deep within.

> "My Father, if there is any way, get me out of this. But please, not what I want. You, what do *you* want?"[51]

Jesus became quiet, as though straining to hear God whisper his divine will. Then he stood to his feet. The front of his robe was stained with dirt and grass. He walked back to where he had left Peter, James, and John, only to find all three fast alseep.

He knelt and shook Peter's shoulder.

> "Can't you stick it out with me a single hour? Stay alert; be in prayer so you don't wander into temptation without even knowing you're in danger. There is a part of you that is eager, ready for anything in God. But there's another part that's as lazy as an old dog sleeping by the fire."[52]

Jesus left his friends—not once but twice more—to go pray. Each time he cried out the same words, "My Father, if there is no other way than this—drinking this cup—I'm ready. Do it your way." Each time he returned to find his best friends sleeping.

On his third return he woke them with the words, "Get up! It's time to be going! My betrayer is here. The Son of Man is about to be handed over to the hands of sinners."

My doggy ears had already picked up the intruders' noise. Jesus and his disciples were no longer alone in the garden. Serpents were slithering in.

FAMILY DISCUSSION

1. How do you think Jesus felt when he was praying for God to take away the trial he was facing?
2. How do you think God felt when he had to tell his Son that he needed to face it?
3. What do you suppose gave Jesus the courage to say "yes" to his Father—even when he knew it meant he would have to suffer and die?

SCENE 205

JESUS IS ARRESTED[53]

While Jesus was still speaking, the sounds of snapping twigs and marching feet grew louder—probably even the humans could hear them. I bet they could smell the perspiring people, too. Moonlit faces emerged from the darkness, and we saw a sickening sight—Judas leading a mob and wearing a plastic smile.

Judas, the former *disciple*. Judas who had sat around hundreds of campfires listening to Jesus teach about his Father's kingdom. Now he was the lead face in a posse of sword-and-club-wielding men. Judas had changed sides. And he was about to turn the King of the universe over to representatives of the prince of this world—a band of chief priests and Pharisees.

"Hail, Master!" Judas said through his smiling mask.

"Your master is *from* hell, all right!" Pete snapped.

"Shhh!" Priscilla warned.

Then Judas grabbed Jesus by the shoulders and kissed him on the cheek.

"Yuk!" Pete cried. "I'd rather be kissed by a mad dog. No offense, girl."

When Judas pulled his head back I could see tear streaks on Jesus' face. And just for a moment a sad cloud appeared in the lost disciple's eyes.

The lynch mob stepped forward. Two men with fiery eyes grabbed Jesus. As they held him tightly Jesus said to his fake friend, "You would betray me, Judas, with a kiss?" Jesus' voice was broken. He seemed more concerned with the vise-grip around Judas' soul than with the hands encasing his own body.

Mr. Pilgrim was restraining Pete with a tight grip on his shoulder. But there was no one to hold the disciple Peter back.

In an instant Peter produced a sword that he had hidden beneath his robe. He sliced a *swoosh* through the night air and also through the ear of one of the men holding Jesus. (The man—now with only one ear—was Caiaphas' slave.)

Priscilla shrieked in terror and I cut loose barking. I couldn't help it.

The mob behind Judas sprang into action, drawing swords and raising clubs. But before anyone could shout, "Attack!" Jesus stooped down and picked up the severed ear. He was as serene as if he were alone in the garden, picking up a feather for closer inspection.

He turned to Peter and said,

> "Put your sword back where it belongs. All who use swords are destroyed by swords. Don't you realize that I am able right now to call to my Father, and twelve companies—more, if I want them—of fighting angels would be here, battle-ready? But if I did that, how would the Scriptures come true that say this is the way it has to be?"[54]

Then Jesus turned and faced the man who was now down to one ear. The man's face was contorted in pain and his neck was red with blood. He was using both hands to press against the wound on the side of his head, but his fingers were ineffective dams.

Jesus smiled a kind smile and took a step forward. The man drew back. Jesus nodded his head and reached out toward the man. He gently touched his hands, and the wounded man reluctantly moved them, exposing the deep gash.

Priscilla gasped. So did Pete.

Jesus placed the severed ear over the wound. He removed his hand and the ear stayed put. It turned from gray to pink. The crowd joined Priscilla and Pete in a giant gasp. I could feel my fur standing on end.

Then turning to the priests and Pharisees, Jesus spoke.

> "What is this—coming out after me with swords and clubs as if I were a dangerous criminal? Day after day I have been sitting in the Temple teaching, and you never so much as lifted a hand against me. You've done it this way to confirm and fulfill the prophetic writings."[55]

But neither Jesus' words nor miraculous action had a softening effect on the mob. Their hearts must have been rock hard with anger and fear. "Take him!" a fancy-robed priest shouted. "He's an enemy of God."

"You don't even know how to spell God!" Pete snapped. "Probably would spell it D-O-G. No offense again, girl."

"Actually, they spell it M-E," Jesna whispered.

Immediately Jesus was grabbed and bound, and then marched away. Jesus' closest friends turned and ran into the night like scared rabbits.

As everyone was leaving—in opposite directions—we remained in the garden. The man with a newly attached ear and blood-soaked robe was still there, too. He looked left and then right—at the backs of the departing mob and the feet of the fleeing disciples. He looked confused, as if he didn't know which way to turn.

He searched his soul for a while longer, then turned and followed after the crowd. Like them he was still a slave to Caiaphas. Jesna sadly watched and then began to talk.

"Tonight you have seen a dramatically different conclusion to the old story of temptation in the garden. Even if the disciples and the high priest's slave haven't gotten it yet—they will.

"Tonight you have seen Jesus reenact the garden temptation faced by Adam and Eve. It's one that every human being will face in their lives—many times.

"But instead of choosing to act independently of his Father (as Adam and Eve did), he chose to obey willingly. He didn't say, 'I choose *my* will.' He said, '*Your* will and not mine be done!' And then he acted on those words.

"Right now it may look like the snake has won again," Jesna said while glancing in the direction of the departing mob, "but it's over now. The blow Jesus struck tonight will be fatal. He went back to the garden and did it right. He chose obedience. Even obedience unto death. The Tree of Life will soon be in full bloom again. But first you will see the tree as a cross."

FAMILY DISCUSSION

1. How do you think Jesus felt when Judas kissed him on the cheek?
2. How would you describe the similarities between Adam and Eve's choice in the Garden of Eden and Jesus' choice in the Garden of Gethsemane?
3. Talk about the most difficult time you have ever faced in choosing between God's will for your life and your own will.

SCENE 206

JESUS BEFORE THE SANHEDRIN (THE HIGHEST JEWISH COURT)[56]

We stood in silence for several minutes. I guess Jesna wanted to let her words about the two gardens sink into our hearts.

When she finally said it was time to follow, Pete sent me off with a "sniff 'em out, girl!" It was like saying "sic 'em" to a ... well, to me. I was off in a flash. The Pilgrim party began jogging along behind. Jesna was bringing up the rear.

"Whew," Pete said after we'd covered the length of two football fields. "Slow down, girl. I'm about to have a cardiologist back here."

"Why don't we drive?" Priscilla asked.

"Because we haven't been more than a mile or two away from the temple courtyard since we got back to Jerusalem last week," Jesna explained. "Besides, it's not that much farther to Caiaphas' house."

"Isn't that where we were when Judas was given those silver coins?" Mr. Pilgrim puffed.

"That's right," Jesna said. "The gang that seized Jesus are taking him to Caiaphas' house. That's why his slave—the man who had the, uh, ear surgery—was in the garden tonight. He was representing the high priest—as his strong arm."

It wasn't long until I was sniffing my way across the courtyard stones at Caiaphas' house. Even though it was almost dawn, the courtyard was filled with people. Some of them were wearing metal skirts and using long spears as walking sticks.

But the trail continued. It stopped inside the same large room where we had seen Judas show his true colors and pick up the money for the "hit" on Jesus.

"See?" Jesna said. "The religion scholars and leaders have been assembled here all night. They sent out the smaller group to go bring Jesus back to stand trial before a kangaroo court."

"Huh?" Pete said, and then began scanning the room with his eyes. "I don't see any kangaroos."

"There aren't any kangaroos, Pete," Jesna explained. "That just means it isn't a *real* trial. These men don't intend to see justice done. They know the outcome before they've even started."

Jesus was standing in the center of the room. He was facing a row of black-robed priests. They were leering at him as if he were the vilest criminal. He did not return their gaze but stared continually at the floor. His hands were tied behind his back with thick ropes. Another rope encircled his arms and chest.

Pete couldn't stand it any longer. "You black-robed jerks!" he screamed. And then he raced to Jesus' side and started trying to untie his hands.

"Don't be afraid, Jesus," Pete said. "I'll untie these ropes while you get a SWAT team of angels down here on the double. They'll get us outa this."

"It's OK, Pete," Jesus whispered. "It's got to be this way.

You go on back with your folks and we'll talk about those angels later—when *you* need them."

Pete obeyed. But not before giving one of the men standing next to Jesus a sweeping hologram kick to the shin.

People in the room were beginning to step forward and make up bad things about Jesus. But we knew none of what they were saying was true. After all, we've been right by Jesus' side for the last thirty-three Bible years.

Finally two men came forward and began speaking about something that had really happened. "That man said," accused one of the men in a hateful tone, "'I can tear down this temple of God and after three days rebuild it.'"

Caiaphas bolted out of his chair and pointed a finger at Jesus. It was trembling with rage. "What do you have to say about that!?"

Jesus was silent. He never broke his gaze at the floor.

"Tell 'em!" Pete shouted. "Tell 'em it's you and your Dad's house and you can remodel it whenever you want to."

Silence remained in the room. Seconds were ticking by like the clock on a time bomb.

"Why doesn't he tell them he was talking about his body?" Mr. Pilgrim asked. "Why doesn't he say he meant he will raise his body—the temple of God's Spirit—back up after three days?"

"They just wouldn't understand," Jesna said. "That would be a foreign notion to them—God on their insides. Plus, that's not the way God wrote the script."

Caiaphas' face was beginning to resemble a ripe tomato. "I c*ommand* you by the authority of the living God to say if you are the Messiah, the Son of God!"

Jesus raised his face to meet the glaring eyes of Caiaphas. It was as if two beams of angry energy were pouring from the high priest and boring into Jesus. But Jesus was in no hurry to answer. After a moment he calmly spoke. "You yourself said those words. You yourself stated my true identity. And soon you'll see it is true: 'The Son of Man seated at the right hand of his Father, arriving on clouds of heaven.'"

At that Caiaphas' tomato face was squashed with rage. He began ripping his robes and yelling like a madman. "He blasphemed! He blasphemed! We do not need any more witnesses! He has accused himself. You all heard him blaspheme! Are you going to stand for such an offense to the Holy God?"

Immediately the crowd of religious leaders began to chant "Death!" And several cried out, "The death sentence for the blasphemer!"

Then many of the religious leaders—priests, scribes, elders, and Pharisees—marched by Jesus and spat in his face. Some struck him with their fists and yelled, "Go on—prophesy, Messiah! Who hit you that time?"

Mr. Pilgrim had dropped to his knees. He was restraining Pete with a bear hug. Mrs. Pilgrim and Priscilla were locked in a wailing embrace. Jesna held me by my collar as I barked out my rage.

Our friend Jesus, the Son of God, God himself, was allowing his Creation to beat him with their fists and spit in his face.

"What are his crimes!?" Pete wept. "What is he guilty of?"

"He's guilty of spreading love and truth, Pete," Jesna sobbed. "And those things have been outlawed on this planet ever since the prince of darkness took over as ruler."

FAMILY DISCUSSION

1. What would you have felt like doing if you had been present at Jesus' "trial" before Caiaphas?
2. Why do you suppose Jesus allowed himself to be hit and spat

on—instead of following Pete's recommendation of calling for a SWAT team of angels?

SCENE 207
PETER'S DENIAL[57]

"Come on," Jesna said. "Let's get out of here. It only gets worse and I'm not sure any of us can stand it."

"No!" Pete shouted. "I'm not leaving my friend when he needs me!"

Jesna turned, faced Pete, and put a small hand on each of his small shoulders. "It's awful, Pete. It's a nightmare! But there is nothing we can do to stop history. And as horrible as this is, the worst thing that could be done is to change anything. The future of billions of souls is tied to all that is happening here."

Reluctantly Pete joined the processional of Pilgrims. We filed out the door as Jesus continued to suffer abuse at the hands of the religious leaders of Jerusalem.

"Hey! Peter!" Pete yelled. "Boy, am I glad to see you!"

And with that Pete began to run across the courtyard. There, on the other side of an ocean of flat-stone patio, was Jesus' first catch: Peter.

I'm not sure how Pete had spotted his face so quickly. Peter's round eyes and curly beard were barely visible to me. He was standing at the very edge of the firelight that was flickering out from a large campfire at the center of the courtyard.

I raced ahead of the others and caught back up with Pete as he was trying to latch onto Peter's leg with a tourniquet hug. But the disciple kept standing there looking very worried. Pete's little arms had gone right through Peter's legs. I got there just in time to hear something shocking.

A girl about the same age as Priscilla had turned to face Peter. She was searching his face as if she had seen him before. "Hey," she began, "weren't you with Jesus the Galilean?"

Pete's face went white as he heard the disciple say to the girl, "I don't know what you're talking about."

Pete stepped away from Peter and began to study his face himself. He was probably wanting to make sure this man wasn't a stranger. Sure enough, it was Peter.

Peter began to make his way back to the courtyard gate, looking as nervous as a puppy trying to cross a seven-lane expressway. Before he could find the exit, someone else spoke up. "This man was with Jesus the Nazarene."

Peter turned and faced the pointing finger. A vein had popped up on Peter's forehead. His eyes flashed panic. His mouth began to swear. "I vow, I never laid eyes on the man."

Pete was in tears. "But, Peter, Jesus said you shouldn't swear. Just let your yeses be yes and your nos no. Weren't you listening?"

By this time the other Pilgrims and Jesna had caught up with us. Their faces were as full of disbelief as Peter's was brimming with terror.

As the frightened disciple was beginning to run through the gate, a couple of bystanders stepped in front of him. "You've got to be one of them. Your northern accent gives you away."

Peter jerked his arm away and shouted, "I don't know the man!"

At that precise moment a rooster crowed.

It seemed to serve as an eerie alarm to awaken Peter's heart.

"You remember that, don't you, Peter?" Pete asked. "I bet you remember Jesus saying that you would deny him three times before the rooster would start waking folks up."

From the look on his face, you could tell that Peter did

remember. For a few seconds his pupils were as large as pinballs. Then he wailed in agony and started running.

When we caught up with him he was back in the garden, crying at the very spot where Jesus had wept through the night.

Pete and Priscilla knelt beside him.

"Don't feel bad, Peter," Pete tried to reassure him. "I was a little scared, too. Jesus will forgive you. And then we'll show the world a thing or two. You and me. You just wait. You'll see. We'll start building churches for Jesus."

But Peter could not hear the words of comfort, and his bitter tears continued to spill on the ground.

FAMILY DISCUSSION

1. How do you think Peter felt when the people in Caiaphas' courtyard started pointing at him?
2. How do you think he felt when the rooster crowed?
3. Have you ever been afraid to be identified with Jesus?
4. Does it make you feel better to know that one of the most important Christians in the history of the world felt the same way?

SCENE 208
JESUS DELIVERED TO PILATE[58]

"Come on," Jesna said as she gave Pete and Priscilla quick pats on their shoulders. "We've got to get back inside the city walls. Peter will feel better soon. And right now, it's time to be with Jesus. He's being taken to Pilate."

"Great!" Pete shouted. "A pilot is just what Jesus needs right now. Why didn't you tell me somebody would be swooshing him outa here?"

"No, Pete, not a *pilot*. He's being taken before Pontius *Pilate*. That's the name of the Roman procurator ... uh, government official, in charge of this part of the empire."

"The sun hasn't been up for thirty minutes yet," Priscilla said while inspecting the horizon. "Does Pilate always go to work this early?"

"No," Jesna answered. "The chief priests and the elders are taking the chance of getting Pilate's dander up by sending representatives to him this early in the morning—to ask for a hearing."

"Pilate has dandruff?" Pete mused out loud. "Maybe you could give him some of your Head and Shoulders, Dad. That stuff keeps your head from snowing—pretty much."

"Ump, hmm," Mr. Pilgrim cleared his throat while using his eyes to tell his son to zip his lips.

We fell in line behind Jesna as she set a course that would bring us back inside the city of Jerusalem. As we walked she began to tell us a little more about Pilate.

"Pilate is the fifth Roman official to rule over Judea in Jesus' lifetime. He has been in charge for the last three years and will rule for about seven more."

"I thought the head Roman ruler lived up in Caesarea," Priscilla interrupted.

"That is where his official headquarters are located," Jesna said. "But Pilate has been sent to Jerusalem for a few days to keep order during the Passover celebration. Rome is always concerned that there might be an uprising of the people—especially when so many get together for religious feasts and celebrations."

"I bet Pilate can afford to stay in the best hotel in town," Pete offered. "Dad usually makes us stay at a Motel 6 when we're on vacation. But I bet Pilate stays at a fancy place where you get free shampoo and M&M's on your pillow at night. You know, the kinda place with the thick, fluffy towels you can't see through."

"Pilate stays at Herod's palace when he's in town, Pete," Jesna said. "But we'll be meeting up with him at the praetorium."

"Is that like a chapel?"

"Hardly, Pete," Jesna said. "A praetorium is a temporary judgment hall. Pilate uses a large room in Herod's palace as a courtroom. When we see Jesus again he'll be standing before Pilate, who will be both the judge and jury."

"Will that mean ole Caiaphas be there—with his mean ole friends?" Pete asked. "'Cause if they are, I can't be held responsible for my actions."

"No, Pete. Those very same folks—who don't have a problem with hitting and spitting on Jesus—won't enter the praetorium."

"Are they afraid of Pilate?" Priscilla asked.

"No," Jesna responded. "They think it will make them unclean—unholy—to be in a gentile court. And that would mean they couldn't participate in the remaining feasts of this holy week."

"Wait a minute," Pete said while shaking his small head from side to side in disbelief. "Those mean ole priests and elders can lie, cheat, and spit on God's Son right in the face, but they won't walk across Pilate's playpen?"

"That's right, Pete."

"Wow," Pete continued. "Some people sure have funny ideas about what's clean and what's dirty."

"You've said a mouthful, little disciple," Jesna replied as we continued to walk back toward Jerusalem.

"Jesus was right," Pete went on. "Some folks just keep

straining at dust specks while gulping down sewer water."

"You know it's OK to stop with just being right, little brother," Priscilla said. "You can save the color commentary."

FAMILY DISCUSSION

1. What do you think are the best ways to become clean and holy—on the inside?
2. What are some things you can do to participate in that process?

SCENE 209
THE DEATH OF JUDAS[59]

The sun had pushed away from the horizon and was floating freely in the morning sky. Its dawn rays were no longer blocked by the rolling hills and were now spray-painting the walls of Jerusalem with the rich colors of daybreak. But there was a strange chill in the morning air. I could feel it all the way down my back and into my heart.

When we were about one good frisbee toss from a city gate, Pete let out a yelp. "Oh my!" he wailed. "What is that hanging from the tree?"

I quickly looked around to locate the source of Pete's distress. But before I could, Priscilla did. "Oh no!" she gasped. "It's not a *what*. It's a *who*!"

There, about seventy-five yards to the right, I saw it. A man was slowly swinging from the limb of a tree. A rope was stretched around his neck, his body lifeless. A small crowd was forming around the grotesque scene.

Mrs. Pilgrim had already pulled Priscilla's head to her chest. Mr. Pilgrim had put an arm around Pete's shoulder.

"It's Judas, isn't it, Dad?" Pete asked.

"I think so, Son," Mr. Pilgrim answered somberly.

"What happened?" Pete questioned. "Did some of Jesus' friends get to him?"

"Oh no," Jesna spoke up. "A true friend of Jesus would never do that. Judas hanged himself. And not very long ago. Let's go on inside the city now. I'll tell you what happened as we walk."

We continued our slow procession toward the city gate. Jesna began to tell us the last chapter from the story of Judas.

"You see," she began, "Judas didn't go back with the mob that took Jesus from the garden last night. I guess he couldn't get over the look in Jesus' eyes—after he kissed him. His heart began to fill with guilt.

"He staggered through the garden for a few paces—behind the gang. Then he went off by himself, fell on his face, and began weeping for what he had done. After a long cry, he raised himself up and ran to the temple—at the crack of dawn. He entered the courtyard and burst into an area where some priests and elders were sitting. Seeing some of the same faces present when he had taken the silver, he cried out, 'I have sinned in betraying innocent blood.'

"'What do we care?' a high priest said. 'That's your problem now.'

"Hearing that, Judas threw his coin pouch at their feet. The silver pieces went in thirty different directions. Judas went in just one. He ran from the temple, found a rope, and hanged himself—as you saw."

"What happened to the money?" Pete asked.

"The priests will use the thirty pieces of silver to buy a plot of ground for a 'Potter's Field'—a burial place for the homeless. It will come to be known as the 'Field of Blood.'

"And as difficult as it may be to believe, Jeremiah the

prophet saw this hundreds of years ago. He wrote, 'They took the thirty silver pieces, the price of one priced by some sons of Israel, and they purchased the potter's field.'"

Pete strained his neck to look back at Judas. "Do you think Judas will make it to heaven, Jesna?"

"That's in God's hands, Pete. But right now we need to catch up with Jesus. He's been placed in the dirty hands of Pilate."

FAMILY DISCUSSION

1. Judas and Peter both did something for which they were very ashamed. But they lived their lives very differently afterward. Take a moment to ask God for the grace to always respond to your mistakes like Peter, instead of Judas.

SCENE 210
THE TRIAL BEFORE PILATE[60]

We made our way through the narrow streets and wide-open spaces of the city of Jerusalem. I was becoming pretty familiar with the place. Shoot. You could probably drop me off in any corner of the city and I could find my way back to the main gate—without even using my nose.

Jesna led us right through the middle of a gang of high priests and elders who were clustered around the doorway to Herod's palace.

"They won't go inside," she whispered.

"I know," Priscilla said.

"Pardon me, boys," Pete said while strolling through Caiaphas' midsection. "I know you all have to stand outside so you won't be getting any dirt on your souls, although I don't know how anybody could tell. It'd be like putting a smudge on a pig's back."

"Come on, Son," Mr. Pilgrim said while tugging on Pete's elbow.

We walked across shiny marble floors and between polished stone walls. Herod's palace was filled with artwork—a lot of which were sculptures of people with big noses and metal shirts.

Our journey ended in the middle of a large, windowless room. A man wearing a white robe and leaves on his head seemed to be in charge. Jesna told us he was Pilate. After a few minutes Jesus was brought in. His arms were tied behind his back and his face was marked by blood.

Pete ran to his side. His parents didn't try to stop him.

Pilate took a long gaze into Jesus' kind eyes and seemed to become flustered. He marched out of the room without saying a word. I ran to follow him—to hear all the details—while the Pilgrims and Jesna stayed with Jesus.

Pilate walked to the front door of his house and spoke to the high priests as if they were naughty children. "What accusation do you bring against this man?"

A priest answered back in a timid voice. "If this man were not an evildoer, we wouldn't have disturbed you—especially not at such an early hour, good governor."

"Then take him yourselves," Pilate barked. "Judge him by your own law."

"But it is not lawful for us to put anyone to death," a gang member said.

Pilate spun on his leather sandals and marched back to the praetorium. He split the middle of the judgment hall with quick strides and stepped back up onto a wooden stage. "Are you the King of the Jews?" he sneered at Jesus.

"Is this what you believe," Jesus began, "or did others say it to you about me?"

"Am I a Jew?" Pilate shouted at Jesus. "Your own nation and the chief priests have handed you over to me. What in the world have you done?"

Jesus returned a tired, gentle smile for Pilate's rage. He said, "My kingship is not of this world; if my kingship were of this world, my servants would fight, that I might not be handed over to the Jews; but my kingship is not from this world."

"Wow!" Mr. Pilgrim said. "He's talking about the kingdom right until the end. It must be real important that people know what it is and how it is so different from this world—the one ruled by men."

Pilate's expression had softened a little. Perhaps he was intrigued that someone would speak to him with such certainty and conviction—when he was holding his life in his hands. He spoke crisply, but with less anger in his voice. "So you *are* a king?"

Jesus studied the floor before answering. "You say that I am a king. For this I was born. For this reason I have entered into the world, to proclaim the truth. Everyone who is of the truth hears my voice."

Pilate paused for a moment. Then he snapped, "What is truth?"

Jesus did not respond.

"The truth," Jesna whispered, "is that the front door to Eden is open again. All who will hear are invited to come back home and live—in God's kingdom-garden, on earth now, and in heaven later. But you have to be willing to die to yourself and this world to get in."

"Yeah," Pete whispered back, "and you have to be willing to live by the King's rules, huh?"

"Right."

But the truth was not sinking into Pilate's head. He marched back through the room without saying another word. I stayed right by his side to see what he would do next.

When he arrived at the front door to the palace he spoke angrily to the priests. "I find no crime in this man."

But the mob of religious leaders became urgent in their demands. They said, "No! He stirs up the people. He teaches throughout all Judea, from Galilee even to this place."

With that Pilate again set sail for his courtroom. I thought I saw a dark cloud of fear in his eyes. This time, when he arrived back at the praetorium, he stopped in front of Jesus. Looking into his Maker's eyes, he said, "Where are you from?"

Jesus did not answer.

"If he says heaven, Pilate will just think he's crazy, huh?" Pete said.

Silence grew in the room until it filled every inch of space and pressed against Pilate's patience. He shattered it with a booming voice. "You will not speak to me? Do you know that I have power to release you and power to crucify you?"

Jesus raised his head and looked Pilate squarely in the eyes. He said with a sad, calm voice, "You have no power over me that is not given to you from above. Because of this, those who delivered me to you have the greater sin."

Pilate appeared stunned. After a few moments passed, he collected himself and went back to his front door to tell the Jewish leaders he intended to release Jesus. This caused an outcry. "No! If you release this traitor you are not a friend of Caesar. Don't you know that anyone who proclaims himself to be king sets himself against Caesar?"

Hearing this, Pilate instructed two of his servants to bring Jesus. He took Jesus by the arm and ushered him outside the palace. The high priests and elders retreated as if Jesus were a rabid dog.

Jesna and the Pilgrims had returned with Jesus, in time to hear Pilate proclaim in a loud, booming voice, "Behold your king!"

The mob held their hands to their ears and began to cry out, "Away with him, away with him, crucify him!"

Pilate shouted over their wails, "Shall I crucify your king?"

To this the chief priests answered from the depths of their dark hearts, "We have no king but Caesar."

As the pandemonium continued to echo outside Herod's palace, Jesna leaned over and whispered, "You might want to note—this is the day of Passover. The fate of God's own Lamb is now sealed."

FAMILY DISCUSSION

1. How do you feel about Pilate for the way he is handling Jesus' trial?
2. What is the threat that Jesus poses to the priests and elders?
3. Has Jesus toppled the rule of all but himself in your heart?

SCENE 211
JESUS BEFORE HEROD[61]

As the mob outside of Herod's palace grew louder, the color began to drain from Pilate's face. Jesus was standing beside him with his eyes closed, head downturned, and arms bound.

Pete was holding one of Jesus' blood-streaked hands and shooting laser beams into the angry crowd with his eyes. If Jesus had wanted a fight, I knew of four Pilgrims, a tour guide, one dog, and ten thousand angels who were ready to help. But he didn't.

I looked up at Pilate as a sparkle lit his eyes and color began to bleed back into his face. I could almost see a light bulb flash on over his leaf-wrapped head.

"So," Pilate began to say to a man in a white linen robe who was standing close-by, "this Jesus is a Galilean, isn't he?"

The man gave Pilate a quick nod and then his eyes opened wide. His face became colorful, too. They exchanged a nod. Pilate cleared his throat to speak.

"Silence!" Pilate boomed out over the crowd.

The raging flood of anger began to seep back within its human banks.

Pilate, still using a thundering voice, declared, "This man is a Galilean. He's not *my* problem. This is Herod's affair. I'll send your *fake* king before your *real* king." With that, Pilate nodded to two soldiers who were standing behind Jesus. They each put a hairy hand under Jesus' arms and pulled him along behind Pilate—back inside Herod's palace.

We followed close behind as Pilate led the way over a sea of shiny marble we had not crossed before.

"Psst, Jesna, where we going?" Pete asked.

"We're going to Herod's chambers—on the other side of the palace. He's in Jerusalem, too, for a few days. A national celebration like the Passover Feast often brings the king and the governor to town—to show that Rome means business about keeping the peace."

"Yes," Mr. Pilgrim said, "I can see why they would be nervous about the possibility of another 'exodus' during a celebration like this."

"You're exactly right, Mr. Pilgrim," Jesna said. "But they'll never guess what's about to happen."

"Huh?" Pete asked.

"Jesus," Jesna began, "is already leading the way to the greatest exodus imaginable—out of sin, death, the grave, and away from the rule of the prince of this world."

"We call it Easter, huh, Jesna?"

"Right, Priscilla."

We turned off the hallway and entered a great stone chamber.

"Hey!" Pete exclaimed. "I know that fat guy with the crown on his head. He's the one who put John the Baptist to death. But what's he doing in this place?"

As Jesus was being led across an immense stone room Jesna whispered an explanation.

"That is Herod Antipas. He came to power after Herod the Great, who died when Jesus was only two years old. Herod Antipas is in charge of Galilee and Perea, but he has strongholds in several places. Machareus, which is south of Jerusalem and east of the Dead Sea, is where he was staying when he ordered the death of John the Baptist."

"Who's in charge of Judea and Samaria?" Priscilla asked.

"At first (before Jesus was a teenager)," Jesna said, "it was Archelaus Ethnarch."

"That's a mouthful," Pete said. "How would you like to have to call *him* in for dinner every night, Mom?"

"Then," Jesna continued, "Judea and Samaria came to be ruled by Roman governors—such as Pilate. But listen. Herod Antipas is about to speak."

"Well, if it isn't Jesus. We've both traveled a long way to meet here in your *holy* city."

"I think he's being sarcastic," Pete whispered to Jesna.

"I've been hoping to have an audience with you, Jesus. It isn't often I get to talk with another king."

"Yep, he sure is," Pete said again.

Herod began to pepper Jesus with questions. And he kept trying to get him to perform a miracle—suggesting that Jesus make himself fly or turn the wine in a goblet into water.

But Jesus would not perform tricks. The King of the universe just stood in silence. He refused to become a court jester for the ruler over a small strip of desert.

Eventually Herod lost his patience. Then he lost his temper. He stood to his feet and began to taunt Jesus. "So, do you wish the same fate as that smelly John the Baptist? I can arrange that, you know!"

With his encouragement, the soldiers began to mock and jeer Jesus, too. Quickly the scene began to resemble Jesus' "trial" at Caiaphas' house.

After a while Herod seemed to tire of the sport. He ordered Jesus to be dressed up in an elaborate king costume and then sent him back to Pilate. As we followed Jesus back across the marble sea, laughter from Herod's chambers bellowed out from behind.

"That's OK," Pete said with a sob. "I know who's going to laugh last. Me and Mr. Jesus!"

FAMILY DISCUSSION

1. Why do you think Pilate was relieved to send Jesus to Herod?
2. Why do you suppose Jesus refused to perform miracles for Herod?
3. What do you suppose Jesus was feeling as he stood before the earthly king?

SCENE 212
PILATE DECLARES JESUS INNOCENT[62]

When Pilate saw that Jesus was back in his chambers, he slammed his fist down on a wooden table. Then, with a quick swipe through the air, he motioned for the captain of the Roman guard to come before him.

"Go," he began as the captain stood at attention, "and tell those high priests and religious leaders to stand before my balcony. Tell them to be there immediately. I have some words they need to hear! Some strong words!"

The captain spun on his heels and clanked his way out of the room in rapid step. Pilate pointed to another soldier and said, "Take Jesus to the balcony. Now!"

Jesus, wearing the purple robes of a king and markings of a beaten slave, was led away. We followed behind him. Pilate stayed in his chambers. I looked back to see him pacing, mumbling to himself, and wringing his hands. Clearly, he was perplexed.

Jesus was made to stand close to the center of a large second-story stone terrace. From his elevated position he could see a huge area—outside Herod's palace—filling with people. Soldiers were escorting black-robed priests, elders, and Pharisees to the front row. I recognized the face of Caiaphas and many of his horde.

When some of the high priests saw that Jesus was wearing a purple robe and holding a scepter, their faces began to flash terror. They were doing more pointing than a pack of bird dogs in the middle of a covey of quail.

After a large crowd had gathered, Pilate walked out and sat in a high-backed chair next to where Jesus stood. He studied the faces in the mob for a long while as some unseen hand slowly began to turn up the mob's volume.

When the noise reached the level of a high school football game—after a bad call by an official—Pilate stood. He walked to the marble railing of the balcony and spoke.

> "You brought this man to me as a disturber of the peace. I examined him in front of all of you and found there was nothing to your charge. And neither did Herod, for he sent him back here with a clean bill of health. It's clear that he's done nothing wrong, let alone anything deserving death. I'm going to warn him to watch his step and let him go."[63]

At that the crowd turned into a pack of *rabid* bird dogs. "No! No! You are no friend of Caesar! Traitor! Kill him! If you are a friend of Rome—kill this traitor!"

Not all of the crowd became crazed. As the mob sprayed its venom I saw four wet, brown eyes. Two Marys—Magdalene and the mother of Jesus—were shivering like frightened puppies. Their gaze was locked onto a master who was about to be devoured by the frenzied pack.

FAMILY DISCUSSION

1. If you were standing in the place of Jesus' mother, what would you be feeling while the crowd was shouting for Pilate to kill your son?
2. If you were standing in Jesus' place, what do you suppose you would be feeling?

SCENE 213
JESUS OR BARABBAS[64]

The crowd had become a lynch mob—whipped into a frenzy by shouts of "Kill him! Kill the traitor!" The high priests were feverishly working as black-robed cheerleaders. I looked out over the angry sea of sweat-covered brows, screaming mouths, and billowing dust. There were very few islands of compassion. The religious leaders had seen to that.

Pilate's dilemma was temporarily interrupted. A messenger wearing a thin white robe was tapping him on the shoulder. He handed Pilate a piece of parchment, which was folded in half, and took two steps backward.

Pilate unfolded the document. For the second time that morning his face became ashen. I thought that he was going to faint.

"What'd it say? What'd it say?" Pete asked while craning his neck to inspect the markings on the document. "Pilate looks like he's seen a ghost. He looks like *he's* a ghost."

"It's from Pilate's wife," Jesna began. "She wrote her husband a note that says, 'Don't get mixed up in judging this virtuous man. I've just been through a long and troubled night because of a dream about him.'"

Pilate collected himself and walked to the edge of his balcony. He cleared his dry throat and cried out above the crowd noise: "It has been my custom to release a prisoner during your Passover feast."

A collection of high priests—the most vocal of the cheerleaders—separated themselves from the crowd and drew closer to the base of the balcony. "Yes!" one shouted. "That is your custom!"

"Then which prisoner do you wish for me to release today: Jesus Barabbas, or Jesus, the so-called Christ?"

The band of high priests turned and faced the mob and raised their hands over their heads. They began hollering at the masses, "Ask for Barabbas! Ask for Barabbas!"

"Who is Jesus Barabbas?" Pete asked. "I didn't know there was anyone else in the Bible that had 'Jesus' for a name."

As the high priests continued their march through the crowd, Jesna leaned in and explained. "Barabbas is a criminal. He's been thrown in prison for starting a riot in the city and for murder. Pilate is hoping that even this angry mob won't be able to ask for the release of a murderer. Surely, he wishes, they will ask for Jesus, the Prince of Peace, instead of Barabbas, a murderer."

"Well!" Pilate shouted. "Which do you want me to release?"

Immediately the mob began to scream, "Barabbas! Give us Barabbas!"

Pilate was speechless for almost a minute. When he realized the mob was hellbound, he cried out, "Then what do I do with Jesus who is called Christ?"

They shouted back, "Nail him to a cross!"

"For what crime?" Pilate screamed his objection.

But the crowd just yelled all the louder, "Nail him to a cross!"

The mob was too angry for reason. Pilate probably assumed the obvious—a riot was about to explode. He motioned for a servant to bring him a large basin of water.

In full view of the crowd he dipped both of his arms into the water, withdrew them, and flung water from his arms at the crowd. "I wash my hands of all responsibility for this man's death. From now on, it's in your hands. You all are the judge. Not me! This is on your heads!"

Then Pilate signed a piece of parchment which pardoned Barabbas. And he ordered that Jesus be whipped and turned over to the mob. With that the politically minded governor carved his name deep into the dark side of human history.

FAMILY DISCUSSION

1. If you were a judge and Pilate appeared in your courtroom to be tried for his role in Jesus' death, would you find him innocent or guilty?
2. Is it possible to wash away guilt with a basin of water?
3. How can guilt be washed away from your life?

SCENE 214
JESUS MOCKED BY THE SOLDIERS[65]

Two muscular soldiers grabbed Jesus and pushed and pulled him down a flight of stairs. The descent was from Pilate's balcony to the open courtyard. The angry crowd parted as Jesus was led to a large wooden pole. From our vantage point the opening in the mob looked like the growling mouth of a wild animal. It sounded like that, too.

Jesus' bound hands were jerked up over his head and tied to the pole with leather straps. A bulky Roman soldier pulled back Jesus' dirty robe down to his waist. Jesus' bare back was exposed to the sun and to the angry mob.

Another soldier—one with a menacing face—stepped behind Jesus. A long leather whip was circled through his right hand. The end of it rested in the dirt like a desert snake, ready to strike. The man looked as if he enjoyed his ghastly work.

Pete buried his head in Mr. Pilgrim's side. Priscilla was already using her mother's bosom as a blindfold. Both Pilgrim parents were themselves looking away from the horrible scene. Pilate had retreated inside the palace. I felt a woeful howl trying to escape my throat.

The crowd was not so squeamish. It had become the wild animal it resembled. As I surveyed the faces—yelling with rage, yelling for blood—I saw that the two Marys were being whisked away. The men escorting them, arms draped around shoulders, were hiding their faces. But I recognized them from their clothes. They were two of Jesus' disciples. I think it was James and John.

WHAP! The sound of the leather whip striking bare flesh cracked through the heavy air. It was almost as loud as a rifle blast. I looked at Jesus. A bleeding stripe had been cut into his back by the leather explosion—parting it into a red sea.

I could only see the side of Jesus' face. But his teeth were tightly clenched in pain. The crowd cheered and hollered for more. They got their wish. Thirty-eight more lashes followed the first.

When the scourging finally ended, all four Pilgrims sank to the ground. Their fingers had become white from trying to keep the sounds of the blasts from beating on their eardrums. Priscilla was retching. I thought she was about to throw up.

I looked out over the crowd. By this horrible moment, even the most vocal instigators were looking away. Jesus was hanging limply. His knees were dangling just above the ground, held in midair by the leather straps bound to his wrists. His back was no longer recognizable as belonging to a living human. It was scarlet red. It was raw ground meat.

A soldier threw a clay pot full of water in Jesus' face to revive him. He twitched in pain and pawed at the ground with his feet—trying to stand.

Another soldier cut through the leather straps that ran from Jesus' wrists to a large nail over his head. He cut through them with one blow from his heavy sword. Jesus crumpled to the ground. His knees and elbows became his feet. The crowd had become stone silent. They began to inch even farther away from Jesus—as if he were a leper, as if they were beginning to recognize their guilt.

Two metal-clad soldiers pulled Jesus to his feet, each with an arm under his shoulders. They led him through a door that was directly underneath the balcony where we sat. I watched through two stone posts. Jesus' head was resting almost against his own back.

Jesna stood to her feet and begin to walk inside the building. I was the only one that followed.

We saw that Jesus had been taken back to the large room called the praetorium inside Herod's palace. By the time Jesna and I arrived, Jesus had been stripped of his bloody robe and dressed in a red toga.

"Here," one soldier began in a mocking tone, "I've made a crown fit for a king of your stature." Then with a dark laugh he shoved a twisted circle of thorny branches onto Jesus' head. Immediately blood began to stream down the sides of his face.

"And you should have this," another laughed. A stick, a second fake scepter, was placed in his right hand. And with that the soldiers knelt before him in mocking reverence. "Hail to you, Jesus, King of the Jews!"

Then they rose to their feet. Some filed by and spat on him—as the high priests had done earlier this morning at Caiaphas' house. Another took the stick from his hand and struck him on the head.

When they had tired of their sport, they took the red toga off of him and put back on his torn and bloody robe. "It's time now!" one said. "It's time for your coronation. They should have his throne ready by now."

"Yeah," laughed another. "It's bad manners to be late for your crucifixion."

FAMILY DISCUSSION

1. Please take a few moments for silence. During this quiet time reflect on what the apostle Peter meant when he wrote, "His wounds became your healing" (1 Peter 2:24).
2. Perhaps this would be a good time to whisper a thank you to Jesus, now reigning in heaven, for what he has endured for all of us.

SCENE 215

THE ROAD TO GOLGOTHA[66]

The pack of soldiers took Jesus back through Herod's palace to the open courtyard. Most of the crowd were still there. Judging from their shouts and jeers they had overcome any squeamishness.

The Pilgrims had come down from the corner of the balcony where they had been curled together. Their faces told a sad story. Each had been crying. They joined Jesna and me, some hundred feet from where Jesus was made to stand.

The crowd had found its lost rage. "Make him carry his cross!" some began to shout. That was exactly what the Roman guards had in mind.

Two soldiers hoisted a heavy wooden cross from the ground. It stood above them, about the height of a basketball goal. The wood of the cross was roughly hewn. Long splinters, bent nails, and off-kilter angles revealed that it had been hastily constructed by amateur carpenters.

Jesus was spun so that his bleeding back was in front of the cross. The angled lumber was turned sideways and dropped over his right shoulder. The impact would have sent him to his knees—but two soldiers grabbed him on the way down.

They pulled him to an upright position.

A whip cracked the dusty air. "Now, king! Carry your throne."

The insult stirred the crowd into a chorus of derision. Jesus began to inch his heavy load through the midst of the jeering mob.

Pete had seen all he could stand. He raced over to the back end of the cross. It was plowing a trench into the dust. He bent down and choked out, "H-here, J-Jesus. I'll help you with this." But his hologram hands were of no use.

Within a few yards Jesus stumbled. He fell at the feet of one of the few people who were not screaming insults—a man whose eyes were almost as wet as those of the Pilgrims.

The man's head snapped back as a burley soldier shoved his body toward the crumpled Jesus. "You help him. You look strong and fit."

The man did not hesitate. He knelt down and removed the heavy cross from Jesus' back. "It would be my honor," he whispered to Jesus. A faint smile pulled at the corners of Jesus' lips as the man stood to his feet, his cross now on a new disciple's back.

"Who's that?" Priscilla whispered to Jesna. "I think I read about him in Sunday school."

"That's Simon," Jesna answered. "He's from Cyrene, in northern Africa."

"What's he doing all the way over here?" Priscilla thought out loud.

"There's a large Jewish population in Cyrene. They have their own synagogue. Simon is here to celebrate the Passover. He, of course, had no idea he'd help bear the burden of the Passover Lamb."

Priscilla nodded her understanding.

Simon was now out front, dragging Jesus' cross through the narrow streets of Jerusalem. It was a load even for his healthy back.

Jesus was close behind. It was all he could do to drag himself along. A number of women were following Jesus and crying loudly. They reminded me of the women paid to be out front at a funeral procession.

Roman soldiers lined both sides of the march, keeping screaming onlookers out of the way. But many of these onlookers fell in behind, becoming part of the huge angry mob that was following.

At one point Jesus roused himself and turned to face the wailing women. The Roman soldiers clanked to a stop as Jesus began to speak with a weak voice.

> "Daughters of Jerusalem, don't cry for me. Cry for yourselves and for your children. The time is coming when they'll say, 'Lucky the women who never conceived! Lucky the wombs that never gave birth! Lucky the breasts that never gave milk!' Then they'll start calling to the mountains, 'Fall down on us!' calling to the hills, 'Cover us up!' If people do these things to a live, green tree, can you imagine what they'll do with deadwood?"[67]

"That'll be enough," one of the soldiers shouted. "If you have that much energy you can carry your own cross, king!"

Jesus turned away and the procession continued on. The wails of the women had ended. But the noise of the mob increased, the flames of their fury fanned by Jesus' prophesy.

In a few moments we were marching past the entrance to the temple, where a dead bush stood barren. Pete saw it, too.

"Isn't that the fig tree that Jesus cursed a while back?"

"Yes," Jesna answered. "It is."

"Well, I wish he would curse all them black-robed trouble-makers."

"He did, Pete. When you heard him talking to the fig tree, he was really talking to another pompous growth with shallow roots—the high priests and Pharisees. Soon they'll be dead-wood, just like that fig tree there—just like Jesus prophesied."

FAMILY DISCUSSION

1. Close your eyes and imagine what it would be like to witness Jesus on the road to Golgotha. Now, in your own words, pray a prayer of thankfulness for his willingness to make that trip.
2. In what ways can you be like Simon of Cyrene, assisting Jesus in the load he carries?

SCENE 216

THE CRUCIFIXION[68]

The soldiers led Jesus outside the city walls to a hill called Golgotha. Jesna told us that Golgotha means "the place of a skull." That made a lot of sense. From a distance the side of the knoll looked like a human skull. Pete didn't make that connection. He described the place as "a broken hill."

Simon was told to drop the cross. He did so and it hit the ground with a thud. Simon touched Jesus on the arm and drifted back into the crowd. The dust cloud launched by the cross was wafting behind.

Jesus stood limply beside his cross. He looked as if half of the bones in his body were missing. A soldier dumped the contents of a clay jar into a metal cup. He put the cup to Jesus' mouth. Jesus tasted the liquid and then slowly shook his head, refusing a second sip.

"What's in that cup?" Pete asked.

"It's a mixture of wine and gall. It's a mild pain killer."

"Why won't Jesus drink it?" Priscilla asked pleadingly.

"Yeah," Pete whispered. "I'd gulp down ten gallons of it."

"I don't know," Jesna said. "Maybe he wants the bread and wine he shared with his friends to be the last things to enter his mouth. Maybe he wants to feel *all* of our pain."

At that moment two soldiers shoved Jesus to the ground and then onto the wooden cross.

"Oh no!" Pete shrieked. "Look at the size of those nails!"

With that he buried his face in his father's chest. Mr. Pilgrim clenched his eyes together so tightly white wrinkles appeared at his temples. Priscilla and Mrs. Pilgrim took the same posture, and Priscilla clasped her ears with tear-streaked hands. Even Jesna was staring at the ground.

I hope none of them saw what I saw. I hope none of them heard what I heard. A wild-eyed Roman soldier drove ten-inch nails through each hand of the Son of God. A man, whom Jesus himself had crafted in the womb, was hammering him to a tree—as if he were a Christmas ornament. Jesus accepted his torture without resistance.

A third nail was sent through Jesus' feet. A triumphant shout went up from the crowd. And then the cross went up. It was dropped into a two-foot-deep hole with a flesh-tearing thud. The agony of Jesus' face was mirrored on the faces of the four Pilgrims and Jesna.

As dirt was being packed back into the hole, Jesus began to move his mouth, trying to form words.

"Shhh!" one of the soldiers laughed. "I think the king would like to address his subjects."

"Yeah," began another. "I bet the king is going to cuss out

all of his disobedient servants."

"Father," Jesus began weakly. "Please forgive them. They don't know what they are doing."

An unearthly silence fell on the band of soldiers like a collapsed circus tent. For more than a minute they stood in stillness, tent poles to the canopy of quiet. For a long moment of time that stillness covered the crowd. But their blind anger proved stronger than their guilt.

"Come on!" a soldier shouted, throwing off the silence. "Don't you all start getting soft on me, just because the king refuses to cuss. I've got some dice. Let's see who's going to win the king's robe. Whoever gets lucky can sell it for a week's wages, maybe more."

Eternal life was theirs for the asking. But they would gamble for the value of a week's wages.

As the soldiers began to wager for Jesus' only earthly possession, the crowd looked upon Jesus' suffering with satisfaction. The black-robed leaders seemed pleased with their morning's work. Jesna, the Pilgrims, and I shivered with compassion for our friend's agony.

"Remember," Jesna sobbed. "All is not lost."

Pete and Priscilla both raised their heads to look at Jesna. She was standing in the shadow of Jesus' cross.

"Your best friend there"—no one braved a look—"is hanging from a 'tree of death.' But now it will be, for all time, a 'tree of life.' The gate to the Garden of Eden is about to swing wide open. Jesus on this cross has become a new 'tree of life.'"

FAMILY DISCUSSION

1. Sometimes an event is talked about so much that its emotional impact is diminished. Take a moment to reflect silently on the suffering of Jesus.

2. Reflect further on the notion that Jesus, your friend, would go through all the pain and suffering again—just for you.
3. Pray for the strength to endure the smaller sufferings—your pain that comes from living in but not being part of the world—with the willingness of Christ.

SCENE 217
JESUS DERIDED ON THE CROSS[69]

Somewhere in the whirling nightmare, high-pitched sounds pierced the air. It was metal striking metal—again.

Then I heard two muffled "thuds." It was the sound of wood being dropped into earthen holes. Two more crosses were planted. "Those are the two robbers who are being crucified with Jesus," Jesna whispered. "One on his left and one on the right."

Pete nodded his understanding. But his eyes were still glued to the ground. His lips were quivering.

A rustle began to ripple through the crowd. A path was being cut through the heart of the mob. An official sent from Pilate was walking through the middle of the onlookers, parting them like a knife in soft butter. He walked right up to the soldier wearing the most metal and handed him a thick piece of parchment—about the size of one of Pete's cardboard lemonade signs.

The soldier looked surprised. He quickly nodded. Then he motioned for a ladder to be placed against Jesus' cross. He climbed the ladder himself and hammered the sign to the cross. The impact of each hammer blow sent tremors through Jesus' bleeding body.

The message nailed over Jesus' head read:

JESUS THE NAZARENE
THE KING OF THE JEWS

Before the soldier could put his feet back on the ground, shouts rang out from a black-robed choir. "No!" several of the high priests were loudly objecting as they raced to form a circle around the official. "Don't leave that sign there. It says 'The King of the Jews.' Change it to 'This man *said*, "I am the King of the Jews."'"

The official met their anxious protests with a steely-eyed gaze. It was hard to tell if it was anger (at the priests) or remorse forcing the words out of his mouth, "What has been written, is written."

With those words spoken, he spun and strode away. The black-robed priests were left to stew in the truth—now nailed over the head of Jesus. And just in case anyone might miss Pilate's testimony, the words on the sign were written in three languages—Hebrew, Latin, and Greek.

It wasn't long before some in the crowd—perhaps trying to come to the rescue of the frustrated high priests—began to mock Jesus.

"You bragged," one passerby shouted, "that you could tear down the temple and then rebuild it in three days—we're waiting. Time is running out for you. Show us how fast you can construct a temple—carpenter."

"He was talking about his own body," Priscilla snarled. "And you'll see, all right, in three days."

"Save yourself!" another jeered. "If you're really God's Son, come down from that cross! We're waiting!"

The crowd's insults seemed to please the high priests. Their heavy mood lightened and they began to joke among themselves and with the scholars and leaders.

"Yeah," one mocked, "he saved others? He can't even save himself!"

"If he's 'King of Israel,'" another began, "let him get down from that cross. Then we'll all become his subjects."

"Yeah," said one with the grayest beard. "He was so sure of God—blasphemed by calling him his daddy. Well, where's his daddy now?"

"Up in heaven crying," Pete sobbed. "Just like I'm doing down here. Just like *you'll* be doing in a few days, if you can get your heart back from the devil."

FAMILY DISCUSSION

1. "Hardening one's heart" is a phrase often mentioned in the Bible. This is a condition that a notable Pharaoh and most of the crowd gathered around Jesus' cross seemed to share in common. What do you believe could cause someone who knows about Jesus to harden his or her heart against his truth?
2. Pray and ask God to soften any areas of your own heart that are not completely open and pliable to Jesus' teachings about living in the kingdom in full surrender to the will of God.

SCENE 218
THE TWO THIEVES[70]

Not everyone dressed in black was mocking Jesus. Nicodemus was in the crowd. He had become a fixture on the edge of Jesus' ministry since the night he was almost persuaded to be "born again." And there he was now, still standing on the brink of conversion.

Or perhaps he had finally toppled over the edge and become a believer. He was mopping tears from his bushy eyes with the black sleeves of his Pharisee's robe. He was weeping unashamedly, standing close to a small island of mourners, slightly apart from the angry sea.

Perhaps the Scriptures he always strapped to his forehead when praying (to love God with all your heart, soul, and mind) were finally being written on his heart.

"Hey, isn't that good ole Matthias over there?" Pete choked out.

Pete still hadn't looked up at Jesus. But he had broken his gaze with the ground long enough to spot the thirteenth disciple.

"Yes," Jesna said. "Matthias is here. He's one of the few close followers of Jesus to brave public recognition. He's always been a disciple at heart."

And there were others standing in the island of grief. Mary Magdalene, Jesus' mother, and John, whom Jesus called "beloved," were clustered together.

Mary Magdalene's face was a fountain. She had an arm draped around Jesus' mother to offer support. But it appeared to be Mary, the mother, who was the real pillar. She had been preparing for this day for thirty-three years. She stood tall. But you could see in her dry eyes that she stood with a broken heart.

Jesus must have spotted the tiny island of compassion. He must have spotted his mother. A weak voice sounded overhead.

"Woman," he said, having made eye contact with his mother. "Behold your son!"

Then looking at his beloved John, he said with a trembling head, "Behold your mother!"

"Wow," Pete said, "Jesus is thinking about others, even while he's dying."

"That's right," Jesna spoke, "a widow without someone to look out for her would soon become a beggar in these times."

The Son of God, the Son of Man, was also the loving son of Mary. But the act of grace weakened him. His head fell back to his chest. Mary's eyes were no longer dry.

After several minutes passed, my attention was again called upward.

"Some Messiah you are!" an angry voice rang out from overhead.

I looked up and saw the twisted form of one of the criminals crucified with Jesus. He was bleeding from his hands and feet. A cold sweat glazed his shivering body. He wasn't finished mocking Jesus.

"If you are the savior, then save yourself! Save us!"

Jesus' eyes were closed. His head was downcast. He didn't move one muscle in response to the mocking thief.

But the other criminal spoke up. He rolled his head to the side and stared at the mocker through the tops of his eyeballs across the body of Jesus.

"Have you no fear of God?" he asked in a raspy, gargling voice. "You are getting the same punishment as him. And you deserve it. So do I."

At that Jesus opened his eyes and raised his face. He laid his head to the side and offered his defender a weak smile.

"We deserve this," the man continued. "But not him. He's done nothing to deserve this."

Then the broken criminal said something I'll never forget. He spoke with sincere conviction. He spoke with the same certainty which was in Peter's voice when he proclaimed that Jesus was God's Son.

"Jesus, please remember me when you enter your kingdom."

Jesus let his smile broaden. He said, "Don't worry. I will not forget you. This very day you will join me in paradise."

The thief's eyes opened wide with amazement. He shared a smile with Jesus. In the last moments of Jesus' life as a man, two more were ushered into the kingdom he had come to proclaim. One was a ruling Pharisee. One was a common thief. They were different. They were the same.

And before either had time to entertain a doubt, God spoke. He spoke to them both. He spoke to the whole world. He used the sky. He used sign language.

FAMILY DISCUSSION

1. Which of the two thieves do you most easily identify with?
2. If you picked the good-guy thief, what's keeping you, today, from choosing to be with Jesus in the paradise of his kingdom established on earth?

SCENE 219

THE DEATH OF JESUS[71]

Within moments the clear noonday sky became dark—darker than a solar eclipse—darker than a starless night. God's blackout lasted for three hours. Jesus must have gotten his love for symbolism from his Father, I thought.

As time passed in darkness the tone of the crowd began to change. In the gray-grim face of God's judgment, few dared to continue mocking. Others, who had been crying softly, began boldly proclaiming Jesus' identity. Maybe they felt safer in the darkness. Maybe they felt safer since God had chosen sides.

But, as Pete would say later, "Nobody had seen nothing yet."

Around midafternoon Jesus groaned deeply. Then he raised his head and faced the cold, lonely sky. He cried out loudly,

"Eli, Eli, lama sabachthani?"

Before Pete could ask, Jesna said, "That means, 'My God, my God, why have you abandoned me?'"

"Oh no!" Pete cried. "Jesus must feel awful. He must feel the worst kinda homesick in the universe."

Saying that, Pete braved to look up at Jesus for the first time. "Don't feel that way, Jesus," he comforted. "Your book ain't over yet. I've read some of what comes next. It gets a lot better, real soon. You'll see!"

Pete's parents both gave him a squeeze. Priscilla and Jesna each took one of his small hands into their not-much-bigger ones.

Pete wasn't the only one to show emotion. One of the bystanders stepped forward and said in a high-pitched voice, "Did you hear that? He's calling for Elijah."

One standing next to him ran and soaked a sponge in the pitcher from which Jesus had refused to drink earlier. He stuck the sponge on the end of a stick and lifted it to Jesus' mouth. But another pushed him away and said with a cautious laugh, "Don't be in such a hurry to stop his pain. Let's see if Elijah answers his call!"

A black-robed priest was shaking his head and moving his lips. Even in the darkness his face was white—as if he had seen a ghost. I leaped over to his feet to hear what he was quietly saying.

"Oh my! Oh my! What have we done? He's not calling for

Elijah. He's quoting Scripture. Even now, after all of this, he's quoting Scripture."

Jesus cried out loudly one more time. And then he breathed out—for the last time. The Son of Man, the Son of God, had completed his assignment.

"Mission accomplished!" Jesna choked out.

"Mission accomplished!" Pete echoed.

Then she hollered at us in a surprisingly urgent voice. "Better hit the ground! God's got a giant exclamation point to put at the end of this chapter of his Son's story."

We all followed her advice—and her example. And within half a second of our faces making contact with Golgotha dirt, the skull-hill began to tremble as though it wanted to say something. The city of Jerusalem began to tremble. It seemed that the whole world was groaning.

The sounds of the earth shifting and boulders cracking in two exploded all around us in the darkness. But then, as quickly as it began, it stopped. The world became still again. The sun pushed its way through the canopy of darkness it had been hiding behind and unfurled a cloudless blue sky.

The Pilgrim family and I had been vibrated close to a group of Roman guards—or perhaps they had bounced our way. Each of the weathered soldiers looked as frightened as a helpless child. The captain, a centurion, slowly surveyed the tussled landscape and then the lifeless body of Jesus. "Surely," he began reverently, "the man we killed was God's own Son! A heavenly king!"

"I guess he can't read Hebrew, Greek, or Latin," Pete quipped. "I mean, he's the one who nailed the sign over Jesus' head. I guess some folks just need things spelled out for them in God's sign language."

"You've said a mouthful, Pete," Jesna said. Then she started pulling on his sleeve and pointing straight ahead. "Maybe you've said more about God than you know."

A group of black-robed men were running frantically up the hill. They stopped in front of the high priest.

"Come on," Jesna said. "You don't want to miss this!"

We arrived just in time to hear, "This is awful, Caiaphas! This is just awful!"

"What is awful?" Caiaphas demanded impatiently.

"It's the temple, Caiaphas, the temple!"

"What about the temple!? Was it damaged by the earthquake?" he asked in a panic.

"Oh no. Not one stone was disturbed."

Caiaphas sighed and looked greatly relieved.

"It's the curtain inside!"

Caiaphas' relief was short-lived.

"The curtain separating the Holy of Holies from the Holy Place. It's been ripped in two, top to bottom!"

Caiaphas' face became as white as a sheet.

"What's wrong, big guy?" Pete asked. "You look like you've seen a *Holy* Ghost."

FAMILY DISCUSSION

1. How do you interpret God's "sign language" that followed Jesus' death—the three hours of darkness, the earthquake, and the tearing of the curtain in the temple?
2. Now that you, as a Christian, are allowed to freely enter into God's presence—into the Holy of Holies of God's temple in your heart, how do you use that special access to your Father?

SCENE 220
WITNESSES OF THE CRUCIFIXION[72]

The sun shone brightly. Perhaps it had been refreshed by its midafternoon nap. Witnesses to the crucifixion began to evaporate in its rays, leaving only a few puddles of people behind.

One of those "puddles" included Mary, Jesus' mother, her sister, Mary the wife of Clopas, and Mary Magdalene. The weight of their grief had them on their knees.

I looked over at Pete. His head was in a slow left-to-right motion. First he would look over at the weeping women, and then over, and up, to Jesus. And then back again.

The view became more than Pete could take. "Why did my friend Jesus have to die!?" he blurted out—so loudly that I wondered if he was asking God.

"Why!?" he shouted and then buried his head in his mother's side. Yep, it was God he was addressing.

A long silence followed. Jesna broke it.

"Pete," she began softly. "Your question is one that theologians will be asking—and trying to answer—for centuries to come.

"Some will say that Jesus died as a 'ransom' price for the sins of man. Some will say he represented all mankind and died as a 'substitute,' died in their place. Some will say a 'satisfaction' was required to be paid—because God's righteous character required death as a judgment on sin. And others will claim it was to provide victory over all evil and hostile powers."

Pete let an angry look take over his face. "Well, which is it!?" he asked impatiently. Pete wasn't impressed with theologizing. He was always more interested in experiencing theology than talking about it.

"Well, Jesna," he said again, in a tone marbled by his frustration. "What's the goodest reason my friend had to go and die?"

"All of the reasons I mentioned are good. All of them are correct. But there *is* another good reason."

Pete rolled his face away from his mother's side. He looked at Jesna through bloodshot eyes, sucked in a strong, sniffling inhale through his runny nose, and said, "OK, I'm listening."

"Behind you, Pete," Jesna began, "is the most important symbol ever chosen. And it was chosen by God himself. It's the cross. It summarizes mankind's spiritual goal."

"Huh?"

"Imagine," Jesna continued, "that the beam which runs up out of the ground—pointing toward heaven—represents God's will, his plans, and desires for your life.

"Now imagine that the beam which runs parallel to earth represents man's will, plans, and desires—what *you* want to do regardless of God's desires.

"Notice that the two pieces of timber run in opposing directions. The will of God is very often at odds with the will of man.

"But, Pete, the heart of Jesus is at the center of where the two beams meet. The heart of Jesus, his essence, his life, rests over the place where the two boards occupy the same space.

"You remember how much Jesus wanted to avoid death, don't you? You remember that he cried out three times for his Father to take all this away. But in the end he always said, 'Nonetheless, your will, Father, and not mine be done.'

"Jesus is our example. He is the example of how we are to say, 'Nonetheless, Daddy, God. Your will and not mine be done. Realign the beams. Make my will the same as yours, Father. Make my heart a place where your desires and mine are one and the same, a place where the crossing of wills is uncrossed.'

"This cross where Jesus died is the ultimate symbol of how we are to solve our 'at-odds-ness' with God. We are to imitate

Jesus. We are to imitate his example of obedience—even unto death."

"But that seems impossible," Priscilla said.

"Yes!" Jesna went on with a broad smile. "It is completely impossible for a human being to do. It can only be done by inviting Jesus to come and live inside of you, to do it for you, through you. That is why the Last Supper, Holy Communion, will become such an important part of Christian life."

"Yeah," Pete said with a sly smile. "He's already done it. It's a piece of cake for him now—to help us do it."

"And," Jesna echoed, "do you know what happens when you are willing to die to your own will—your 'apart-ness' from God?"

"What?" Pete asked.

"Easter."

FAMILY DISCUSSION

1. Are you aware of any areas in which your will, plans, and desires are running crossways to God's? Reflect on these areas of your life.
2. Then ... ask Jesus to be fully present and alive in your heart—working to help you conform your will to that of your heavenly Father. This is bearing your own personal cross.

SCENE 221
JESUS' SIDE PIERCED[73]

The lifeless body of Jesus hung above us—the first crucifix, the last sacrificial lamb. He had poured out his life in obedience to his Father. He had poured out his blood to spring-clean a dingy world.

Muffled sobs from the last group of mourners were low notes drifting in the background. Measures of high-pitched clanking from the soldiers' swords and armor played at a closer range.

"So," Priscilla asked, "that's why Jesus had to die, so we would learn to imitate him?"

"He died to set you free from the grip of the world, the flesh, and the devil, so you would be *free* to begin imitating him," Jesna corrected. "But there is one more story I'd like to tell you about why Jesus came to live with us and why he allowed himself to die."

The Pilgrims all handed Jesna their attention. I sat back on my hind legs to better enjoy the story.

"Once upon a time ..."

"I love stories that start that way!"

"Shhh, Pete!"

"... there was a little boy who had saved his money for a long, long time—to buy a puppy. He had saved almost a dollar."

And I really love puppy stories. Reminds me of my own puppyhood.

"He went to a pet store and pressed his nose against a big glass puppy pen. He looked a little like a pig—with his nose flattened by the glass—as he inspected the puppies.

"The pet store owner saw the little boy—at least his face—and walked over to help him. 'Looking to buy a pup today, Son?'

"'I sure am,' the little boy said proudly. 'I've been saving my money and I've got all this here. It's almost a dollar. I want to buy me one of your puppies. How much do you want for one?'

"The owner was smiling. 'Well, you're looking in the right pen. Those are my cheapest puppies. They're not full-blooded.

But I'm asking fifty dollars apiece for them.'

"The little boy dropped his smile. So did the owner. Then the boy spoke up and asked, 'What if I give you all this money now, then bring you a dollar a week until I've paid for it? I can make a dollar a week cutting grass—if my daddy will let me.'

"'Well, that sounds like a pretty good deal to me,' the round-faced owner said. 'Which one have you got your eye on?'

"'That one right there,' the little boy said, pointing to the far corner of the glass pen.

"As the little boy was pointing, the smallest puppy stood up and started hobbling toward the finger that was aimed at him.

"'Oh no,' the owner objected, 'you don't want *that* puppy. You can see he was born without a hip socket. He can hardly walk. I'm going to have to put him to sleep.'

"'Please don't put that puppy to sleep,' the boy pleaded. 'He's the one I want. He's as good as any of the rest, maybe better. I'll give you a hundred dollars for him—if you don't mind waiting a hundred weeks.'

"'But he's not worth a hundred *pennies*, he's ...'

"The pet store owner suddenly became quiet. The little boy had hobbled back from the glass cage. Two crooked legs and a set of shiny braces were in plain view.

"'He's worth every bit as much as any of the rest,' the little boy said, his face puckered with conviction. 'I don't walk too good myself and my parents tell me I'm worth as much as anybody else on earth.

"'Besides,' the boy continued as a tear was sliding down the owner's face, 'he's going to need somebody who will understand what it's like.'

"So the owner sold the crippled puppy for full price. It was worth a million dollars to the boy—and he to the puppy."

Even Priscilla was crying after that story. But it was Pete who asked the first question.

"But, but, what's that story got to do with Jesus coming to earth?"

"Because, Pete, Jesus knew that we would all need somebody who could understand what it's like to be a human being. And he knew we needed someone to tell us we are valuable—and to buy us back."

As the Pilgrims were nodding their heads in somber understanding, a splashing sound was heard. I looked up and saw that blood and water were running down from Jesus' side. A burley soldier was withdrawing his sword.

FAMILY DISCUSSION

1. What did Jesna's story mean to you?
2. What is a pain or difficulty in your life right now? How does it make you feel toward Jesus to know that he can "understand" all human pains?
3. Perhaps the two of you (you and Jesus) would like to talk for a while about what it's like to be human and how he can help you with your pain.

SCENE 222
THE BURIAL OF JESUS[74]

After a long time of silent reflection, Jesna urged us to follow her back inside the city walls. Pete gently touched Jesus on his ashen feet and gave the bottom of the cross a bear hug before leaving.

When we were about halfway between Golgotha and a city gate, I looked back to where Jesus' lifeless body hung. The skull-like structure of the hill looked even more ghastly in the dying daylight. It caused ripples to run through my fur ... and *I* know how the story ends.

"What!" Pete yelped, nearing the end of our walk. "Why are we going back inside Pilate's place? I hate it in there!"

"It's a real special scene that God wrote into Scripture. You really need to see it."

We crossed the marble floor of the great room in which Pilate was seated. The stone felt cool through the pads of my feet. It would have been a good place for a nap.

"Who's that man in the black robe?" Pete asked angrily.

"That's Joseph. He's a rich man from the town of Arimathea, northwest of Jerusalem, and a member of the Sanhedrin (the Jewish high court)," Jesna answered.

"What's he doing here? Gloating with Pilate?"

"No, Pete," Jesna answered. "He's not like many of the others in the Sanhedrin. He's a righteous man, a seeker after the kingdom. He and Nicodemus have been secret disciples of Jesus."

"Yeah, well, why didn't he start whopping Caiaphas upside the head?"

"For fear of the others, Pete. Even your namesake—Peter—knew a bit of cowardice before coming to his senses."

"I guess God's midnight-at-noon display may have helped revive his faith," Priscilla suggested.

"Maybe so. But whatever the cause, it's burning brightly now."

We arrived to hear his conversation with Pilate just as Joseph was asking for permission to bury the body of Jesus.

"Is he already dead?" Pilate mused out loud.

Then he summoned for the centurion who was in charge of the crucifixion to ask him that question. Pilate didn't know about the centurion's recent statement of faith.

The centurion arrived and told Pilate that Jesus was dead. He said that he had seen blood and water run from his side, proving that he had died.

At that Pilate gave Joseph permission to take Jesus' body down from the cross for burial.

We followed Joseph as he walked somberly back to the cross of Jesus. When we arrived we found that Nicodemus was already there. Two of his servants were carrying large sacks that smelled of strong perfume.

Jesna told us the bags contained a hundred pounds of myrrh and aloes mixed together. Nicodemus walked behind the two servants. He was carrying a pure white linen burial shroud and a heavy heart.

The two men set the sacks of ointment on the ground. Using the same ladder as the soldiers had, one climbed up beside the cross and began the gruesome task of bringing the body of Jesus back down to the very earth he had created.

Nicodemus and Joseph spread the linen shroud over the ground. They poured spices on the cloth, then placed the body of Jesus on the linen. They poured more spices on top of his body. Jesus looked like a man half buried in sand at the beach. My emotions didn't match the image. Jesus was then wrapped from head to foot with the shroud.

Seeing Jesus' face covered caused a sickening feeling to bubble in my stomach. Judging from the color of the Pilgrims' faces, they were feeling it, too.

Joseph, Nicodemus, and the two servants placed Jesus' body on a wooden bier that had been lying nearby. They hoisted God's Son to their shoulders in one smooth motion. A few soldiers were still standing close-by. They neither taunted nor offered to help.

The world's smallest funeral procession began. A couple of

the women from Galilee (I could only clearly make out Mary Magdalene) followed behind the raised bier. We fell in behind them.

The sad march did not last very long. Nearby was a garden, and in the garden a tomb hewn from rock. Jesna said that it was a new tomb—one in which no one had ever been lain. She said that it belonged to Joseph of Arimathea.

They placed Jesus on a stone bed and poured more spices on top of the shroud—pulling the linen tightly against Jesus' face. As we backed out of the tomb the rock walls echoed with our sobs.

Then Joseph, Nicodemus, and the two servants rolled a giant stone in front of the entrance to the burial cave. It was taller than Mr. Pilgrim and twice as fat.

As we slowly walked away, Jesna whispered, "Don't think of that place as a tomb. Think of it as the womb of God's new kingdom on earth. It won't be long until the new birth."

FAMILY DISCUSSION

1. Why do you think Joseph and Nicodemus were willing to take such a risk to be kind to Jesus?
2. What do you think Jesna meant by calling the tomb a "womb of God's new kingdom on earth"?

SCENE 223
THE GUARD AT THE TOMB[75]

We all walked aimlessly outside the city walls until after sundown. Even Jesna seemed to have lost her sense of direction.

I'm not sure if it was by accident or design that we eventually stumbled upon our time car. It had been sitting in an olive grove—abandoned—since shortly after Jesus' final entry into Jerusalem.

Jesna stepped behind the panel of gauges and buttons. We followed behind like zombies—taking our familiar seats. Even Pete's face showed no excitement as Jesna began punching buttons and twisting gauges.

She caused the car to ascend straight up through the night air. Then she turned a sharp left and began speeding toward the glowing city of Jerusalem. If we had been on the ground, I'm sure gravel and sand would have been sprayed everywhere as Jesna "peeled off" at whiplash speed.

Whoosh! went the thick wall of Jerusalem as we sailed right through it. We raced down one of the city's widest streets faster than a greyhound dog could bound over them. The torches blipped past us like stripes on an open freeway.

Whoosh ... whoosh ... whoosh! went each of the thinner walls of Herod's palace, like the fanning pages of a book. Jesna brought us to a neck-extending stop just inches in front of Pilate and a band of black-robed Sanhedrinites.

"You stopped too soon for me," Pete said through puckered lips. "I wish you'd flattened them religious leaders!"

"Sir," a man wearing the fanciest black robe began.

"Kiss-up!" Pete snapped.

"A serious matter has been brought to our attention concerning that liar Jesus. While he was still alive, he claimed he would be raised from the dead after three days. Well, actually, he said, 'Destroy this temple and I'll raise it up in three days.' But some of his followers have taken it to mean he was referring to his body."

"Your point," Pilate snapped.

"Well, we've been talking ..."

"Yeah," Pete began, "and every time you all talk you make the devil smile."

"Pete!"

"Sorry, Mom."

"... and we've come to the conclusion that the tomb Jesus is in should be sealed until the third day."

"So, you think this Jesus might make good on his promise?" Pilate said with a worried look.

"Oh no, Pilate! We're just concerned that some of his disciples might come and steal the corpse and then go and tell everyone who'll listen, 'He's risen from the dead.' If that happens we'll be worse off than before—and so will Rome. As a final deceit, it would surpass the first—his claim to be God's Son."

Pilate wrinkled his chin and nodded his head. "You'll have a guard of Rome's elite soldiers," he finally said. "Go ahead and secure it the best you can."

That brought beady-eyed smiles to the faces of the black-robed men. They thanked Pilate vigorously and made a rapid exit.

Jesna put the car in reverse, spun it around, and backed over Pilate's foot.

"Good one, Jesna!" Pete exclaimed.

We drove toward Jesus' tomb at the speed of a depressed human walking. We arrived only moments before the high priests and their gaggle of goons.

They wasted no time. The tomb was sealed and secured

with military precision. Burley armed guards were posted on either side of the boulder that blocked entrance to the crypt.

It would take a Jonah-out-of-the-whale's-belly miracle for anyone to get into that tomb. God knows what it would take for someone to get out. God knows.

FAMILY DISCUSSION

1. Why do you suppose the religious leaders were so concerned that Jesus' tomb be sealed and guarded?
2. Why is it good for our Christian faith that guards were stationed by the tomb?

SCENE 224

THE WOMEN AT THE TOMB[76]

We backed into a first-century parking spot by the side of Jesus' tomb. From our vantage point we could see the soldiers and their campfire—in front of the tightly sealed grave-vault. We could also see Jerusalem sleeping in the distance.

The sounds of the soldiers' sandals crunching on sand, their deep laughter, and the clinking of their metal skirts punctured the night air with military regularity. But it wasn't enough commotion to keep the Pilgrims from resting their eyes. In fact, Mr. Pilgrim and Pete began to rest their eyes really loudly. Boy, can those two snore!

Not long before dawn of the new week's first day, the ground suddenly began to tremble and shake. It was as if the whole earth had become a giant bowl of brown jello. The earth-jostling awoke the sleeping Pilgrims. They each began to shout as though they were on a roller coaster at Daffy World.

After the earth stopped grumbling, a loud thud was heard. And then a light, brighter and whiter than anything I had ever seen, began to shine out of the open tomb as if it were a nuclear-powered lighthouse. The beam of light was even brighter than the one that had crashed into our car when this ride first began, if you can imagine that. And the fur-bleaching light just kept pouring out of the tomb.

Soldiers began to run every which way—including into each other. As the light began to dim so did our fear. We piled out of the car for a closer inspection. And there was quite a sight to be inspected.

The stone that had been plugging the entrance to Jesus' tomb was lying on its belly. And sitting on its back was the hugest man I had ever seen. He must have been ten feet tall. He was wearing light like a glowing overcoat—and the light was as white as snow.

"Hey, that's Gabriel!" Pete shrieked. "How's it going, Gabe? Nice work with the boulder. Let me know if you need any help standing it back up."

Gabriel said nothing but smiled a warm angel smile at Pete.

The braver guards—the ones who had not already cut and run—stared at the angel as if he were death-about-to-explode in their faces. Their knees were having their own earthquake.

Then when Gabriel disappeared with a *poof!* so did the remaining guards—in the direction of Herod's palace. We stood alone, staring at the open mouth of Jesus' tomb.

Within a few moments we heard footsteps approaching from behind. I turned around and let out a bark. I couldn't help it. I was startled.

But the footsteps belonged to a familiar face—Mary Magdalene. When she got close enough to see that the stone was toppled, her mouth resembled the entrance to the cave. But it wasn't nearly so empty. She began to scream. Then dropping her basket of spices, she turned and ran back toward

Jerusalem.

"Peter! Peter!" she screamed as she ran through the dust the soldiers had stirred up. "Someone has taken Jesus!"

Before you could tree a cat, two men were running toward the tomb. One of them was Peter. I couldn't make out the other one. But he passed Peter on the straightaway and bolted to the entrance of the tomb. He poked his head inside and then pulled it right back out. "He's gone!" he exclaimed. "There's nothing in there but a shroud—an empty shroud!"

In his excitement Peter pushed his smaller friend aside and entered the tomb. We all shot in behind. In the early rays of dawn I could see the white linen that had wrapped Jesus, now lying crumpled on the stone floor in the sun's morning spotlight. I wondered to myself if the particles floating in the stream of light were angelic dust.

On the stone slab where Jesus had been placed, a kerchief was neatly folded. Someone, or some angel, had taken the time to fold the kerchief that had draped Jesus' head.

"He's alive!!!" Peter shouted at the top of his lungs. The tomb became a megaphone, blasting the news to the world.

"He's alive!!!" Peter roared again. Then he and the other disciple darted from the empty cave and flew down the path to Jerusalem. Through a circle of light we could see their sandals spraying sand higher than their heads.

Tears were streaming down Mr. and Mrs. Pilgrim's faces. Pete and Priscilla grabbed hands and began to dance around in a circle. Jesna was looking on—beaming with joy. Not having a dance partner, I began to chase my tail until I'm sure I looked like a blurry circle of fur.

When my batteries ran down I collapsed on the stone floor. Pete and Priscilla had already landed. Then, as we breathed deeply, Pete panted out what we all were thinking.

"May God have mercy! He did it!"

"And," Jesna echoed, "if he was right about this, he was right about everything else he said, too."

"May God have mercy!" Mr. Pilgrim said.

I think God already did.

FAMILY DISCUSSION

1. If you had been with Peter and the Pilgrims in the empty tomb, what would your emotions have been doing?
2. Some theologians have been overheard proclaiming that the resurrection of Jesus was the most important event in human history. Do you agree? If so, why?
3. What does it mean to you to have a live-in Savior who has already overcome sin, death, and the grave?

SCENE 225
JESUS APPEARS TO THE WOMEN[77]

We walked out of the empty tomb to the sounds of a woman sobbing. Before my eyes adjusted to the light, I could smell that it was Mary Magdalene—she always smelled great. At first I couldn't tell if she was crying sad or happy tears.

But then she walked right through us to the entrance of the cave, and as she passed it was easy to tell she was sad.

"What's wrong with her?" Pete asked. "Doesn't she believe Peter, that Jesus is reconstituted? That she's here for the world's first Easter sunrise service?"

"Not just yet, Pete," Jesna said. "Faith comes a little harder for some than for others. But for Mary, you could say, it's on the way."

Mary Magdalene stopped and stooped—to look inside the tomb. Seeing that Jesus was not there, she began to cry more loudly. Then she gasped most of the air right out of the cave.

Pete and I darted over to where she stood trembling like a weeping willow in a windstorm. We looked inside. Two angels were now sitting where the body of Jesus had lain, one where his head had been and one in the place of his feet.

"Oh man!" Pete exclaimed. "Where did they come from? There weren't any angels in there just a second ago. I'd've seen 'em for sure."

Pete had a point. It's hard to miss a couple of giant beams of light when you're in a small, dark place.

"Woman," one of the angels began in gentle, reassuring tones. "Why are you crying?"

Mary answered in an unsteady voice, the edges of her robe aglow with angel-light, "Because someone has stolen away the body of my Lord, and I don't know where they've taken him."

Having said that, Mary turned around and started to walk away—as if talking to a couple of angels was no big deal.

She walked with her eyes glued to the ground and gravity tugging at her tears. And she almost walked right into a man who had suddenly appeared from nowhere. He had a strange glow about him, too, almost as bright as the angels' clothing.

"Woman, why are you crying?" the man asked.

"Mister," Mary said while still staring at her own dusty feet, "if you took my friend, please tell me where he is. I want to care for him."

"Mary," the man said. And there was something very familiar about his voice.

Mary must have heard it, too. She slowly raised her eyes to

meet his. "Teacher!" she exclaimed and then threw her arms up to embrace him.

"Jesus!!!" Pete shrieked. "Look, everybody! It's Jesus!!"

Jesus had taken a step back from Mary's reach. She had hugged only the air where he had stood. Jesus' radiant face was flashing excitement. His mouth issued a caution. "Better be careful, Mary. Better not cling to me right now. I haven't yet ascended to my Father. You go now and tell my friends and disciples, 'I am ascending to my Father and your Father, to my God and your God.'"

Like the disciplined disciple she was, Mary immediately obeyed. She went off running, screaming as she raced, "I have seen the Master! He's alive!"

Jesus threw back his head and laughed the most wonderful, joyous laugh I'd ever heard. It echoed across the dusty hills and valleys. It bounced off the walls of Jerusalem. It was the laughter of winning a marathon and finding your lost child all rolled into one.

Then Jesus lowered his head and looked over at us. "It's done!" he said as a tear welled up in his left eye. "All the things I heard my Daddy whisper to me have come true! Now all who will follow me can leave the devil's prison and join me in kingdom life!"

Oh my! That sent tears sliding down five sets of fleshy cheeks and one furry set. Pete joined Jesus in another giant belly laugh.

FAMILY DISCUSSION

1. What would you do if Jesus suddenly appeared in your home and told you that he would help you defeat the world, the flesh, and the devil, and live an abundant life?

2. Well, you might as well get on with it. Since Jesus is omnipresent, he is in your home, and in you, right now.

SCENE 226
THE REPORT OF THE GUARD[78]

"Let's hop back in the car," Jesna said. "We've barely got enough time for me to show you what happens next—without having to do any backward time leaps."

I'm still not sure I understand skipping across time. But I definitely remember the last time we jumped backward—we almost drowned in the Red Sea. So I was the first one back in the car.

When everyone was belted in place, Jesna pulled down on a lever that jolted us forward. She steered us over the footpath that led from the graveyard of caves to one of Jerusalem's city gates, gaining speed as we went.

Pete seemed to take delight in turning each rock-bump and gully-dip into an occasion for a loud "ouch!" I think he was wanting Jesna to offer him the steering wheel. It didn't work. I guess she still remembered Moses and the Red Sea, too.

We made our way through the massive gate and across the much smoother streets of the city. It appeared that most of the city was still sleeping. But enough sidewalk cooks were awake to fill the air with the delicious smells of baking bread and roasting meat.

"Pete," Jesna said playfully, "you're only a few more Bible days away from hot dogs and cotton candy." Pete's tongue shot outside his mouth and started lip licking, north and south.

It wasn't long until we were passing over the giant expanse of temple courtyard. A few early-morning black-robed worshipers were scattered around. They stood out against the sandy white stone lawn like spots on a Dalmatian.

Jesna parked the car next to a two-story stone structure adjacent to the temple. I recognized it as the place where the Sanhedrin met—when they weren't huddled at Caiaphas' house.

We climbed out and followed Jesna through the thick stone walls. Inside there was a strange mixture of hues. A few red-and-brass-uniformed soldiers stood line to line with a row of black-robed high priests. It reminded me of a football game Pete snuck me into once when I was a puppy.

When we got within earshot I could hear the frantic tones of the lead guard's voice. And I recognized his face.

"I swear by Caesar that's what happened. The earth began to tremble—like right after the crucifixion. Surely you felt it, too. Then the stone came crashing down—it's a miracle none of us were killed. That's when the inside of the cave began to glow like a thousand campfires. But the light was white, like a cloud.

"After that we started running. I don't know what anyone else was thinking, but I was expecting to see Zeus himself at any moment. I thought a giant foot was about to come crashing down on me.

"We went off in all directions, but a few of us ended up together close by your temple here. That's when we decided we should come and tell you what we saw and to ask if you think we should tell the governor."

The black-robed religious leaders went off to a corner for a private huddle. After some animated discussion—with hands pointing in many different directions—all but one returned to where the soldiers stood. The one took a detour. He went and dipped his hands into a large basket filled with coins—just like the one from which Judas' bribe was fetched.

The lone priest filled a leather pouch with the contents of the basket. The soldiers were looking on intently. Then the priest rejoined the crowd gathered at the center of the room. Every one of the soldiers' eyes were glued to the jingling leather container.

"Yes," a priest began, "you go to Pilate. But don't tell him that ridiculous story you amused us with. He'll never believe you. I know I don't! Pilate will assume you were all drunk.

"Tell the governor instead that Jesus' disciples came during the night while you slept and stole the body away." Then the "treasurer" handed over the leather pouch to the lead soldier.

The head priest continued. "If Pilate gets angry at you for falling asleep, we know how to calm him back down." The priest gave a slow, knowing glance in the direction of the coin basket. "He'll not punish you. We'll see to that."

The soldiers bowed to the priests, took their bribe, and left the room.

"That was important for you to see," Jesna began.

"You mean because there's something that soldiers and Sanhedrinites agree on?" Pete wondered.

"No, Pete, it's important because there will be many who lack the faith to believe in miracles. They will begin to spread the story the soldiers are about to tell Pilate."

"I don't know how anyone lacking in faith could believe that," Priscilla began, punching her wrist computer on for the first time in days. "Believing that a few scared-as-rabbits disciples could get past one hundred burly soldiers—with swords and spears—cause an earthquake, topple a boulder, and escape with a body, all before a single soldier could wake up, well—"

"Well," Pete interrupted, "I'm not sure Abraham, on his best faith day, could muster that much conviction."

"Right, Pete," Priscilla said. "That's exactly what I was thinking."

FAMILY DISCUSSION

1. What do you think about Priscilla's and Pete's conclusion about the story the soldiers told Pilate?
2. Aren't you glad it takes less faith to believe in God than to be an atheist?

SCENE 227
THE ROAD TO EMMAUS[79]

"Come on," Jesna said. "Back in the car."

Pete ran over to kick one of the high priests on the shin—as was his custom. But his foot found no more resistance than a shadow would afford. He ran to catch up with the rest of us, grumbling as he came.

"You've got the justice side of Jesus' teaching down better than the love side, huh, little brother?"

Pete's only answer was a pouched-out lip.

"It takes a while for a hologram to become a holy-gram," Jesna giggled.

She must have been in a real frisky mood. Because after saying that she took us on a course that blasted right through almost every stone wall in the city and then right through the middle of a hillside.

"Whoa, Jesna," Pete giggled. "I think I saw some gold back there inside that baby mountain. We might want to go back and pick it up."

"Yeah," said Mrs. Pilgrim, regaining control of her breathing. "Why are we going *through* stuff today, instead of over and around … Oh! Whew!!" she exclaimed while passing through the tangled branches of a giant olive tree.

"Oh, sorry, folks," Jesna said. "I'm just feeling great today. You'll see why soon. We'll all be hearing an old friend teach from the Bible in just … about … NOW!"

As Jesna was saying "now," she hit the brakes and we came to a head-throwing stop, inches behind the behinds of a couple of men who were walking down the middle of a wide road. They appeared to be deep in conversation.

"Cool!" Pete said.

"Sorry," Jesna replied to the rest of us. Then she whispered, "I didn't want you to miss any of this."

"Where are those two guys headed?" Pete whispered back.

"To Emmaus," Jesna answered in a more normal voice. "Emmaus is a village about seven miles northwest of Jerusalem."

"Who are those two?" Priscilla asked. "I can only see the backs of their heads, but they look familiar."

"They're a couple of Jesus' disciples," Jesna answered.

Then all of a sudden a third man appeared—from out of nowhere! He had popped in a couple of paces behind the others, who still were not yet aware of his presence. But we sure were. His sudden appearance snapped the four Pilgrim heads and my own back toward Jerusalem. I think Jesna was expecting him. Her head hadn't moved.

"What are you discussing so intently as you walk along?" the new arrival asked. That sent the two disciple heads in startled motion. Then they stopped in their tracks and faced the stranger. His back was still to us, though. And he wore a hood which was pulled forward so they couldn't see his face.

When the disciples recovered from the shock of the sudden

intrusion, their faces became long and sad, as though they were at their best friend's funeral.

"Are you the only one in Jerusalem who hasn't heard what's happened during the last few days?"

"That's Cleopas talking, right?" Pete asked.

"What's happened?" the new arrival asked.

The men turned toward Emmaus and began walking again. The stranger stepped in between them. They began to catch him up on the latest news.

"I'm referring to what happened to Jesus the Nazarene," one began.

> "He was a man of God, a prophet, dynamic in work and word, blessed by both God and all the people. Then our high priests and leaders betrayed him, got him sentenced to death, and crucified him. And we had our hopes up that he was the One, the One about to deliver Israel. It is now the third day since it happened. But today some of our women have completely confused us. Early this morning they were at the tomb and couldn't find his body."

"I know!" Pete shouted. "I saw the whole thing!"

"Shhh, Petey! They can't hear you, and I want to hear them," Priscilla said with a nudge to her brother's ribs.

> "They came back with the story that they had seen a vision of angels who said he was alive. Some of our friends went off to the tomb to check and found it empty just as the women said, but they didn't see Jesus."[80]

"Well, I understand that a Messiah can be hard to recognize," the stranger said in a surprisingly playful tone.

"Hey," Pete said. "That man's voice sounds familiar!"

"Pete," Priscilla said, shaking her head from side to side. "You really don't listen in Sunday school, do you?"

The man continued talking to the two disciples. "He can be especially difficult to recognize if people become thickheaded or slow-hearted. Take you two, for instance. Why is it difficult for you to see that things had to happen as they did? The Messiah had to suffer and only then enter into his glory."

Then the man became an animated Sunday school teacher. He began with Genesis and taught his way through the Prophets, pointing out everything in Scripture that referred to the Messiah.

"Jesus!" Pete finally blurted out. "That man is Jesus! The way he teaches everything so plain, that's Jesus for sure! But why is his voice a little bit different?"

No one answered. The three stopped walking. They had arrived at the outskirts of a little village.

It appeared that Jesus was going to continue down a path that led past Emmaus. But one of the disciples said, "Stay and have supper with us. It's nearly evening."

So he continued on with them to a small house in the village. We continued bringing up the rear.

Jesus took a seat at the center of a wooden table. The hood still partially obscured his face. He took bread from the center of the table and blessed it. He spoke from the shadows of the cloth cave made by his robe.

Then he pushed the hood back from his face—revealing the familiar hair and face of Jesus (slightly aglow). He broke the bread and gave it to the two disciples.

At that moment the disciples looked up from the table. Their eyes became like saucers. They recognized their Master. They recognized Jesus as he turned the Last Supper into a first breakfast. Then he disappeared, leaving only his broken body of bread to heal their broken hearts. I bet it would be more than enough.

FAMILY DISCUSSION

1. Did you recognize the "stranger" to be Jesus before the two disciples did? Before Pete?
2. How does it make you feel to know that Jesus is available for walks each day with you?
3. Why don't you meet him for one today? (Or tomorrow if you're already in bed.)

SCENE 228
JESUS APPEARS TO HIS DISCIPLES (THOMAS BEING ABSENT)[81]

The two disciples didn't waste a second. Right after Jesus *poofed* into thin air, so did they. But their exit was easier for us to follow.

First, they bolted out the door. Then they ran back in. They picked up the broken bread from the table. Stuffing some in their mouths and the rest inside robe pockets, they bolted from the room again.

We piled into the car. It was a much shorter trip on the Emmaus-Jerusalem road this time because the two disciples were running and leaping and jogging and giggling the whole way.

"Didn't you feel on fire when he talked to us on the road?" one asked. "And when he opened up the Scriptures for us?" the other answered the question with a question. "And when he broke the bread?"

In what I am sure was a new world record for the 10K

Laugh-and-Run, we arrived back in Jerusalem. The two breathless disciples jogged through a maze of Jerusalem's worst streets before stopping at a roughly hewn wooden door. They both started pounding on it with the fleshy undersides of their fists.

A bench or a table toppled inside the house. Then the door slowly creaked open. A wide-eyed disciple was the reluctant doorman. He looked relieved when he saw who it was. I saw it was a bench that had fallen.

The two Olympic runners raced past their door-holding companion and took center stage by an empty fireplace. We all filed in and took front-row seats. Priscilla said she counted eleven heads—not including ours or the two who were about to explode with the news.

But while they were sucking in big breaths to tell their story, one of the eleven burst out with news of his own.

"It's really happened! The Master has been raised up—Simon saw him!"

The two new arrivals let go of the air they had been holding in and sprayed laughter all over the room.

"What? You don't believe us? You think we're mad!?"

"No! No! We've seen him, too. We were afraid you wouldn't believe us!"

"You've seen him, too?" Simon stepped forward and asked.

"Yes! He appeared out of nowhere and walked with us, right into Emmaus. He taught us from his memory of the Scriptures as he walked. He taught us as only Jesus could."

The room was as silent as the space between heartbeats.

"Then, after we arrived in Emmaus," the heavy-breathing disciple continued, "he broke bread with us. Just like he did last Thursday night, when we all ate together."

While they were talking a man entered the room. The edges

of his robe seemed aglow. But everyone was so taken with the story about Jesus they didn't notice his real presence.

Jesus walked around the group and stood behind the two who were telling their story. When suddenly the talkers saw amazement flashing from the faces of their friends—like ambulance lights—they stopped speaking and looked over their shoulders.

Then they jumped halfway to heaven.

When they landed, the man said, "Peace be with you."

"It's Jesus, again, huh, Jesna?"

"That's right," Jesna beamed.

But the group of disciples wasn't as calm as Pete. They looked as if they were seeing a ghost. Jesus read their faces.

"Don't be afraid. And don't let your doubts drown your faith. Look at my hands."

He held out his hands for inspection. They looked just like Jesus' hands used to look, except there were big wounds where the nails had been driven in. And there was that faint glow around their edges.

"Look at my feet," he urged. Then he pulled up his robe a few inches and showed us his feet. They mirrored his wounded hands.

"See? It's really me. Why would a ghost want to have scarred hands and feet? Plus," he continued, "a ghost doesn't have muscle and bone like this." And after saying that he rapped on the table with his bare knuckles.

The disciples were struck dumb with amazement. Priscilla would probably say that Pete was struck dumber. Several seconds passed in silence before Jesus broke it with a huge laugh.

"Do you have any food here, or do I have to whip something up myself?"

They all laughed with him at that. Then one ran and brought him a piece of leftover grilled fish.

"Nice catch, Peter," Jesus said after he had bitten into the fish. "I'm glad you haven't forgotten everything from your old trade."

"Psst," Pete said, trying unsuccessfully to get Peter's attention. "This might be a good time to ask him about another shot at walking on water."

FAMILY DISCUSSION

1. How would you feel if Jesus suddenly appeared at your front door and came inside your house?
2. Then is that the way you feel now? Since he is omnipresent, he's already there.

SCENE 229
JESUS APPEARS TO HIS DISCIPLES (THOMAS BEING PRESENT)[82]

Jesus remained with his friends for a while, laughing and telling stories. But no one was brave enough to ask him where he had been or what he had seen or why his skin seemed to glow—not even the brave little disciple Pete.

Much too soon, Jesus stood to leave. He left everyone with a touch on the cheek and a warm smile. He even had a touch for all the Pilgrims and a pat for me. I'm not sure what the disciples thought about that, since they couldn't even see us.

He walked right through the front door—while it was still closed! "Hmm," Pete mused, "I thought you could only do that if you came from the future."

"Shhh, little brother!"

After he was gone, I felt a mountain-moving faith begin to

grow in my doggy chest. I'm sure I wasn't the only one who felt it.

We stuck around for a while. In fact we stayed so long I began to wonder if Jesna had forgotten that she was still our tour guide. Just as I was about to give her a little bark, the door swung open.

Thomas, the disciple, entered the room in a cascade of sunlight. The door closed. The light left. Thomas stayed. He walked over to the other disciples.

"Thomas!" Simon Peter shouted. "You'll never guess who was just here!"

"Well," Thomas began, "I needn't bother trying, then."

"Oh, come on, Thomas," Pete Pilgrim urged. "It's a fun game to play. I'll give you a hint. He was recently real dead. And now he ain't."

But Thomas didn't appear to be in a mood for fun. He looked defeated, as if he'd just been outrun by an old cat.

"It was Jesus!" Peter exclaimed. "Jesus was here. He talked to us. He laughed with us. He even ate the rest of that fish John cooked."

"Right," Thomas said sarcastically. "And I guess Herod and Caiaphas came over with a roasted lamb for the party."

"He doesn't believe Peter!" Pete said incredulously. "He hasn't got the faith to move a mustard seed—let alone a mountain."

"It's true, Thomas! It's true!" the other disciples began to sing.

Thomas slammed his hands down on the wooden table. "Enough!" he shouted, then looked down at his palms that were now red from hitting the table. But the pain on his face seemed much greater than just from hurting his hands.

"Unless I see the nail holes in his hands, put my finger in

the nail holes, and," he continued as a sob shook his body, "stick my hand in his side, I won't believe it."

"But we saw the nail holes," a disciple said. "He showed them to us!"

"I said ... unless *I* see it!"

The disciples gave up trying to convince Thomas. He could be a stubborn man whenever doubt put a headlock on his brain. Thomas sank down into a wooden chair. He descended even farther beneath the joy the others shared.

Jesna motioned for us to follow her. She walked back outside—following the exact same path Jesus took.

"Ouch! Watch the wall, Sis. Just kidding, you big ole hologram, you."

Back out underneath the sun, we followed Jesna into the car. She began pushing buttons.

"Where we going?" Pete asked.

"Right where we are now, Pete."

"Oh. Well, are we there yet?"

Three sets of Pilgrim eyes bored into Pete.

Then colors began to swirl around us as if we were at the center of a giant kaleidoscope.

"We're traveling eight days into the future, Pete," Jesna said. "But we're not changing locations. And"—as the colors stopped colliding—"Pete, we're there. I mean here."

Pete began to look around—bobbing his head like a hyperactive chicken.

"Look!" he said when his head came to a stop. "It's Jesus!"

Jesus was walking toward us, back to the house where he had been with his disciples.

"Come on," Jesna said. "Let's get inside before Jesus. You don't want to miss the expression on Thomas' face when Jesus walks through the door."

We bolted inside. I barely had time to notice that the band of disciples was sitting around a table. They seemed downcast. Perhaps their faith had been slowly dripping away.

We all spun around and took places against the back wall. In a matter of seconds Jesus came walking through the locked front door. He had a playful smile on his face—as it emerged through the thick wood.

All of the disciples but one leapt into the air with surprise. Thomas was facing away and didn't know what the commotion was about.

Jesus tapped him on the shoulder. Then Thomas joined the other disciples in midair.

"Thomas," Jesus said, after his doubtful disciple had returned to earth. "It's me. Jesus."

I raced around to see the look on Thomas' face. His mouth was open in shock. But his eyes were distant and skeptical.

"Go ahead," Jesus said.

"G-G-go a-a-head and wh-what?" Thomas asked. At an encouraging look from his Master, the disciple reached out his hands to touch Jesus' robe. But they paused—just short of the target—as if the robe were a hot iron.

Jesus raised his hands and rotated his palms toward Thomas.

"Go ahead. Take your finger and examine my hands. And then you can take your whole hand and place it in my side if you need to. I need you to be a believer, Thomas ... not a doubter."

Thomas reached out in a slow, halting motion. The tip of his trembling finger disappeared inside the wound in Jesus' palm.

Thomas fell to his knees. "My Master! My God!"

Jesus reached down and raised Thomas back to his feet.

"You believe because you have now seen with your own eyes, felt with your own hand. That's good, Thomas. But even better blessings are in store when my friends believe without seeing. Because then, they are seeing with *my* eyes and not their own."

Thomas nodded his understanding. Jesus nodded back a huge serving of forgiveness.

"Wow!" Pete exclaimed. "I'm gonna get Jesus to give me some of those magic eyes!"

"He already has, Pete," Jesna said. "And most of the time, you have yours wide open."

FAMILY DISCUSSION

1. Later in his book God will inspire a writer to pen that faith is "the firm foundation under everything that makes life worth living. It's our handle on what we can't see."[83] What are some things about your relationship with Jesus that you believe in—even though you can't see them?
2. What are some obstacles to your faith?
3. Take a few moments to pray that God will shrink all the barriers to your full faith.

SCENE 230
JESUS APPEARS TO THE ELEVEN WHILE THEY SIT AT A TABLE[84]

Thomas sat back down at the table with the other eleven. Faith was leaving no room for doubt on his smiling face.

Jesus surveyed the other smiles worn by all eleven of his friends. They sat around a narrow wooden table. It reminded me of their Last Supper together in the upper room.

Jesus' eyes were like a traffic light. They flashed opposite signals. But not stop and go. He was blinking compassion and frustration, approval and rebuff.

"Thomas is not the only one here whose faith needs help," Jesus began. "Each one of you has seen me since my death. And each of you has heard stories from others who have also witnessed that I am fully alive.

"Yet some of you still question what you have seen—what you are seeing now. (It's not just Thomas who finds it hard to believe.) And why do I say this? Because not one of you is getting on with the important work, work that brought me from heaven to earth—the work of the kingdom.

"So I'll tell you again what I want you to do. I will tell you in plain words.

> "Go into the world. Go everywhere and announce the Message of God's good news to one and all. Whoever believes and is baptized is saved; whoever refuses to believe is damned."[85]

"And," Jesus continued, staring down at Thomas, "if you still need signs, I'll give them to you.

"These are some of the things which will accompany believers: They will throw out demons in my name, they will speak in new tongues, they will lay hands on the sick and make them well.

"Don't be surprised when you, my believers, are so free from fear that a snake in your hands will be of no concern. Don't be surprised if you become so full of my life that you seem almost immune to death.

"My message is serious. My cause is of the utmost importance. You are to preach the good news of the kingdom. You will preach about life and death. The life or death of human souls."

After saying this, the flashing signals on Jesus' face became one—one big warm green light of love for his friends. He held them each in his eyes before leaving the room.

"Go, Coach Jesus!" Pete shouted at the thick stone wall Jesus had used as a door.

"That was the best pep talk I ever heard," Pete went on. "I wish my Pee Wee League football coach could give 'em like that."

"Yeah," Mr. Pilgrim offered with a sly smile, "and I bet you wish he would promise that you could pick up the football without getting tackled."

"Oh yeah, Dad, that would be cool, too!"

"You're sure right about one thing, Pete," Jesna interrupted. "For these eleven players here, it's only half time.

"And," she continued, "there's something else important to know. The 'coach' that gave the speech ... well, he'll be sending in a new quarterback soon."

"Huh?" Pete asked.

"The Holy Spirit, Pete. Rumor has it, he will be impossible to stop."

FAMILY DISCUSSION

1. How would you describe what Jesus was asking his disciples to do? Put it in your own words.
2. What do you think this commission means for you?

SCENE 231
JESUS APPEARS TO HIS DISCIPLES BY THE SEA OF TIBERIAS[86]

Jesna led us back outside. We piled into the car and took off like a helicopter—straight up. We watched over the shiny gold sides of the vehicle as Jerusalem began to shrink. When it became so small I could cover it with one paw, we started traveling north.

We soared toward the green and blue north, leaving the barren brown hills of the Judean wilderness behind. Jerusalem was now a distant postage stamp stuck to a sandy hillside. Jesna was flying due north—against the stream of the Jordan River.

"Where we going now?" Pete asked.

"To the next scene written about in the Gospels," Jesna answered.

Priscilla was looking at her little brother as though he should have known that—as though a monkey would've known.

"I mean, what place?"

"We'll be setting down on a beach," Jesna said.

I liked the sound of that.

"A beach on the shore of the Sea of Tiberias."

And at that, we began our descent. A large heart-shaped body of blue water began to grow in size. When it became so large that there was almost nothing else to see, Pete had a comment.

"Hey, wait a minute. That big ole lake looks just like the Sea of Galilee."

"It is, Pete."

"But you said we were going to the Sea of Tiberias."

"Some passages of Scripture," Jesna began to explain, "refer to it as the Sea of Galilee because it washes up against the east side of the province of Galilee. But it's also called the Sea of Gennesaret, the Sea of Chinnereth, and the Sea of Tiberias."

"I bet that last one is its Roman name."

"That's right, Priscilla. Very good."

"Well," Pete said over a wrinkled chin, "if it had been called the Sea of Caesar, I'd have known *that* was a Roman name."

We touched down, landing to the crunching sounds of metal on sand. But before we had time to inspect the landing site, Jesna turned the whole place into a swirl of color.

"When the colors are spinning clockwise like this, does that mean we are traveling forward in time?" Priscilla asked.

"Amazing," Jesna said as she shook her head from side to side. "Simply amazing. You don't miss a single detail."

"I'm amazing, too. Huh, Jesna?" Pete asked.

Mercifully the spin-cycle stopped before Jesna had to come up with an answer. We found ourselves engulfed by the most beautiful sunrise I've ever seen. Everyone's attention was stolen away. The sea was turning into a shimmering sheet of orange and turquoise, a sheet that was being gently waved in the early-morning breeze by unseen hands.

The sky was also wide awake with color. The bright orange sun was spray-painting the eastern sky with yellows, pinks, and reds. Caught in the mist of color, wispy clouds stood out against the blue backdrop in exaggerated 3-D.

A wooden boatload of fishermen was riding on the slow-rolling waves. The noise of their work arrived in our ears a full second after it had occurred.

And, oh, what a smell! Twelve eyes followed six noses to a fire that was crackling on the beach. A man was roasting fish and baking bread amid the dancing flames. He was wearing a white robe. He was glowing almost as brightly as the fire.

"Hey!" Pete exclaimed. "That's Jesus!"

"Yes," Mrs. Pilgrim said, "it sure is."

"Well, what's going on?" Pete continued.

Jesna fielded the question. "Simon Peter, Thomas, Nathanael, the two Zebedee brothers, and two other disciples have traveled back home from Jerusalem."

"Oh," Pete interrupted, "so they're trying to obey Coach Jesus. He said 'go,' and they've already 'went,' huh?"

"Well, anyway," Jesna continued, "they've been fishing all night ..."

"Still gotta eat, huh, Jesna?"

"... and they haven't caught anything."

"This all sounds sort of familiar ..."

"Pete!" Priscilla snapped. "Will you please let Jesna finish her story!"

Pete poked out his chin but kept his lips together.

"That's about it," Jesna said. "They haven't caught anything, and they're pretty hungry. And a little discouraged."

"Good morning!" Jesus shouted across the water. "Did you catch anything for your breakfast?"

A "no!" came floating back over the colorful waves.

"Then throw the net off the right side of the boat and see what happens."

"I knew this sounded real familiar," Pete said with a very satisfied look on his face. "Better get ready, boys!" he hollered. "Your boat is about to be swamped with fish!"

Ker-splash! The net hit the water on the right side of the boat and briefly stole color from a patch of water. Before the hues could return, busy hands began pulling the net back in.

But the weight of it almost pulled *them* in. For the second time in three years, Jesus had proved he was quite a fishing guide.

Within moments a dirty sail was unfurled and a course set for Jesus. When the boat got within human-eye range, Peter shouted out, "I told you! It's the Master!"

After saying that, Peter started putting his robe back on. He had been down to the bare essentials—for work. He dove into the sea and outraced the boat to the beach. It wasn't much of a contest. The boat was overwhelmed with the flapping catch—153 fish, Priscilla later counted.

Peter arrived at the shore and ran, dripping wet, to Jesus. He gave him a sopping bear hug.

After Peter let him go, Jesus said, "I've got breakfast for you all. You didn't think I'd send you out to do kingdom work on an empty stomach, did you?"

FAMILY DISCUSSION

1. If you were sitting around a campfire with Jesus—after he had cooked you a plateful of fish—what questions would you ask him?
2. Close your eyes and ask him now. What did he say?

SCENE 232
JESUS DOES PETER A BIG FAVOR[87]

It was just like old times—Jesus and his disciples eating fish and bread around a campfire. Their laughter was contagious. Even the Pilgrims broke out with it. I bet enough of it could heal a wound.

The sun inched upward through the morning sky. As it rose it took away the glittering colors from the sea, leaving the watery palette a deep greenish blue. It was still quite a sight.

A gentle breeze kept its fingers in Jesus' hair. The warmth in the wind let me know the day would be a real tongue-wagger for dogs.

After Jesus and the disciples had eaten their fill, he stood, stretched, and walked toward the edge of the water. Peter bolted upright and joined him. Perhaps he thought Jesus was leaving—right across the water. We all crowded in to hear anything that might be said.

With Peter standing by Jesus' side, Jesus rotated his head to face his friend. He looked a little sad.

"Do you think Jesus is mad at Peter for telling those folks he didn't even know him? Or for cussing?" Pete asked.

"You'll see, Pete," Jesna whispered.

"Simon, son of John," Jesus began, "do you love me more than these?"

"Yes, Master," Peter sputtered, "you know I love you."

Then Jesus said, "Feed my lambs."

Peter stared down at the sand. Several moments passed in silence.

Then Jesus asked a second time, "Simon, son of John, do you love me?"

"Yes, Master," Peter said with a puzzled face. "You know I love you."

Jesus said, "Then shepherd my sheep."

More time passed. Peter used it to inspect the horizon and then the sand at his feet. A tear glistened in the corner of each eye. His puzzled face had changed into a portrait of remorse.

Then Jesus said it a third time: "Simon, son of John, do you love me?"

Peter was shaken. His right cheek was now streaked. There was another tear in his voice. He said, "Master, you know everything there is to know. You've got to know that I love you."

"Then, Simon, feed my sheep. Let your love for me have legs and arms. Take care of the ones I have to leave behind.

"And, Peter," Jesus continued, "there's one more thing."

At this point both of Peter's cheeks were wet. He answered, "Yes, Jesus?"

"There isn't room for love and anger in the same heart. I know you love me. I know you will be a responsible shepherd. So let go of the anger you have at yourself for your fear, for denying me. Let it go now, and forgive yourself. I have."

FAMILY DISCUSSION

1. Silently think of something that Jesus has forgiven you for.
2. Now, how do you think Peter felt when Jesus not only forgave him but trusted him enough to give him an important job to do?

SCENE 233
THE ENDING OF MATTHEW: THE GREAT COMMISSION[88]

Jesus walked Peter back to join the others, who were still seated by the fire. Jesus had an arm draped around Peter's shoulders. Peter was wearing it as if it were an expensive fur.

The sun was about halfway between breakfast and noon. The sea had changed shades again. It was now a bright aqua. Its waves had become more angular. Many of them were wearing tiny white caps as they jostled about.

When the disciples saw that Jesus would not be taking a seat with them, they slowly stood to their feet. Following his lead, they clasped hands with their neighbors, left and right. Jesus bowed his head in silent prayer. After a few moments he raised his head, opened his eyes, and announced, "It's time."

The disciples exchanged puzzled looks. They were still wearing them as they all fell in line behind Jesus. He was leading them away from the campfire, toward one last adventure together. The last two disciples suffocated the fire with sand. Any dog would have been proud of how fast they did the job.

We brought up the rear.

"What did he mean, 'It's time'?" Pete asked Jesna.

"He means, Pete, it is time for him to rejoin his Father, at his right hand. It's time for him to ascend to heaven."

"What does 'ascend' mean?"

"Petey," Priscilla broke in, "it means he'll be taking a giant invisible elevator—straight up."

"Oh," Pete said with a fire alarm ringing in his voice. "I'd better run up there where he is. I got a question for him."

I saw something I needed to do, too. It was something I had put off for thirty-three Bible years. It was something staring right at me from the water's edge. A cat! In desperate need of a good chasing!

I was off in a flash, barking like a mad dog and spraying sand behind. The cat turned away from pawing the water for lunch and saw me approaching like the apocalypse in overdrive. It arched its back and let go of a toothy hiss. I kept a'coming. I had it locked in my sights. I pretended not to hear Priscilla shouting, "No!"

The crazy cat wasn't running. Its back just got higher and its hisses louder. It sounded like one of those demon-possessed men before Jesus set him free.

"Prepare for your exorcism, Kitty," I thought to myself as I shifted into my highest gear.

The cat began to move. It leapt through the air, right for my nose. I opened my mouth and ran faster. Then *boom!* But there was no boom. And there was no cat. I raced right through it, *swoosh!* Oh, how disappointing to be a hologram!

But it wasn't without some positive effect. The cat was racing away from the site of our pseudo-collision. It looked like it had seen a ghost dog.

I collected my senses and ran over to catch up with Pete. He was walking by the side of Jesus.

"Mr. Jesus," Pete was saying as I arrived.

"Yes, my little twentieth-century apostle," Jesus answered with a smile. He kept staring straight ahead. I guess he didn't want the disciples to think he was talking to thin air.

"Well," Pete continued, "I was just wondering. Do you still have that rock I gave you?"

"I sure do, Pete. I've kept it ever since you gave it to me for a birthday present." Then he retrieved the rock and presented it to Pete for inspection.

"Wow!" Pete exclaimed. "That's the very same one. It's the smoothest rock I've ever seen."

"Yes. I don't remember ever making a smoother one."

For a moment Pete was speechless. I knew it wasn't a cat that had gotten his tongue. I'd seen to that.

Pete quickly recovered. Boy, did he!

"Jesus, will there be a pond up in heaven for you to skip our rock across?"

"Sure, Pete. There are beautiful pools of water in heaven. But I wouldn't throw our rock away, even to see it skip a thousand times."

"Wow," Pete said, "a thousand-skipper. And I bet you could do it, too.

"But," Pete continued, and then sucked in enough air for a thousand questions. "I was wondering about a few other things, too. Like, do people live in houses in heaven? Will I live with my parents? If Priscilla's there, will it still be heaven?

Where's your house? Do you live in a nicer neighborhood than the angels? Do you have to go to church a lot? (I wouldn't mind too much if you're doing the preaching.) What kind of music do the radio stations play? Can I live in a chocolate house? Can I eat it? Do people still have to go to the bathroom? Will my dog, Wisdom, be there?—she's been real good, I can vouch for that. If people aren't ever sad there, how do they know they're happy…?"

"Pete …"

"Do you ever need Band-Aids up there?"

"Pete …"

"Do you allow baseball, I mean, if you don't hit it toward any windows?"

"Pete …"

"Oh, were you talking to me, Mr. Jesus?"

"Pete, I promise I'll take you on a personal tour someday—a long, long time from now. But for now, just imagine that all the best things on earth are like an out-of-focus copy of what's in heaven. You won't be far off thinking like that."

"Hmm," Pete said. "I wonder what chocolate is a bad copy of. I wonder …"

"Except for one thing," Jesus said. "Real love is the same both places. So the more you stay in love with me, and with your family and friends, the more you'll know about heaven. And the more you'll like it when you get there."

Pete was nodding his little head.

"Now, Pete, I've got a question for you. Would you be willing to tell everybody about my kingdom—the little bit of heaven that's already on earth? Would you be willing to tell them how to get there?"

"Sure I would."

"I knew I could count on you. And the next thing to do will

be to love your parents and Priscilla with your whole heart. I'm going to ask them to do the same special job as you."

Pete was nodding again. "Sounds good to me, Jesus. We'll probably need all the help we can get, huh?"

Jesus gave Pete a pat on the top of his head. They exchanged long, loving looks. Then Pete ran and skipped his way back to his family.

Jesus turned and led his disciples up a barely worn path that wound its way up the face of a baby mountain.

We navigated the steep ascent in single file and arrived at the top. We stood together in a grassy meadow. The sun had not yet completed its own ascent. It sparkled in the sea below like a million floating diamonds. It lit the meadow with bright wavy streaks of green and gold.

Jesus turned and faced his disciples. They gathered around and completed a circle. There was room for us to fill in the gaps, unseen by all but Jesus.

Jesus spoke to us all.

> "God authorized and commanded me to commission you: Go out and train everyone you meet, far and near, in this way of life, marking them by baptism in the threefold name: Father, Son, and Holy Spirit. Then instruct them in the practice of all I have commanded you. I'll be with you as you do this, day after day after day, right up to the end of the age."[89]

FAMILY DISCUSSION

1. What does Jesus' "Great Commission" mean to you personally?
2. How do you feel knowing that Jesus has promised to be with his friends "day after day, right up to the end of the age"?

SCENE 234
JESUS' LAST WORDS AND ASCENSION[90]

After Jesus had commissioned his friends—to go out and proclaim the good news of life in his Father's kingdom—a bright light began to glow over his head. It grew in intensity. Its brilliance caused the edges of a canopy of fluffy white clouds to shine. They looked like they were trimmed with liquid gold.

Shimmering streaks sprayed out from the golden edges in panels of light. What a glorious sight!

The radiant light show wasn't coming from the sun, however. The sun was not yet overhead. It looked on, with wonder and humility, from the sidelines.

The disciples began to stare at the dazzling clouds. Each of them became aglow with the warm golden spotlights that shone down on the face of the sea. But Jesus was not distracted. He continued teaching his friends.

> "Everything I told you while I was with you comes to this: All the things written about me in the Law of Moses, in the Prophets, and in the Psalms have to be fulfilled."[91]

He then gave them a quick tour through the Scriptures, opening their understanding to how all is fulfilled in him, the true Christ. When he had finished the tour through his Father's words, he said,

> "You can see now, how it is written that the Messiah suffers, rises from the dead on the third day, and then a total life-change through the forgiveness of sins is proclaimed in his name to all nations—starting from here ..."[92]

The eyes of each disciple had become locked onto the glowing face of their Teacher. Some had tear streaks, which appeared as long, skinny mirrors of the heavenly radiance.

Then Jesus told his friends that they were the first to hear and see the coming kingdom. He said they were "witnesses." And he instructed them to wait, for a little while, until a special helper (promised by the Father) would be sent.

"Then," he said, "you'll be equipped with power from on high."

With that, Jesus raised his hands and blessed his faithful friends. As he spoke his benediction, the clouds parted. An intense beam of heavenly light came cascading down. It formed a luminous column, a celestial elevator. Then Jesus left, as only the Son of God could do, straight up in holy light. Message delivered. Mission accomplished.

The heavenly table would be set for three. The faithful Son was coming home.

FAMILY DISCUSSION

1. How do you think the disciples felt when they saw Jesus ascend into heaven? How would you have felt?
2. Picture in your mind what that reunion must have been like, when Jesus and his Father saw each other face-to-face.

SCENE 235
A TRIP ACROSS THE GOSPELS AND THE ENDING OF MARK[93]

The disciples stood, mouths gaping, as Jesus soared and faded into the beam of light. Their mouths were still collecting dust when the heavenly lights disappeared—as if sucked up into the sky by an invisible vacuum cleaner.

Pete's and Mrs. Pilgrim's faces stayed glued to the sky. Pete raised his hand and began to slowly wave goodbye.

After a while the disciples exchanged hugs and "can you believe it!!!" expressions. Then they began to descend the hill. They had a rendezvous to get to—with the third member of the Trinity. Witnessing Jesus' ascension had left little room for doubt.

The Pilgrims remained behind. We all enjoyed several minutes of sacred silence. It was Pete who broke it. "I guess it's back to Daffy World, huh?"

He didn't sound very enthusiastic. In fact, for someone on his way to roller-coaster rides and foot-long hot dogs, he sounded downright sad.

"Not just yet," Jesna said. "We've got a couple more stops to make first. Let's get back in the car and I'll explain."

We all followed her as she began to navigate the path of the disciples. Pete crawled up in his father's arms and kept his eyes on the sky as we walked. Knowing Pete, he was probably hoping that Jesus would poke his head back through the clouds and give a thumbs-up sign.

"We're going to travel a few decades into the future before going all the way back," Jesna said. "You've all just seen how Luke ended his Gospel (with the ascension of Jesus). Right before that you saw how Matthew ended his—with the commissioning of the disciples.

"But now I want you to see John putting the finale on his Gospel. (Along the way I'll tell you about Mark's ending.) And then I have one last stop—a special treat—before we, uh, have to say goodbye."

"Jesna?" Priscilla said.

"Yes?"

"I've always wondered. Why did God arrange for us to have four Gospels? Why not just one longer one?"

"That's a good question, Priscilla. Let me try to answer it with a little story.

"Imagine that four kids were trying to watch a baseball game through a knothole in a wooden fence. Each of the four was a different shape and size. Not only did they have to take turns seeing the game, but they also had to twist and bend their bodies a different way to look through the hole. The only thing they had in common was love for baseball and empty pockets.

"One day the owner of the team was driving by. He saw the four fans, pushing and shoving and twisted like a pretzel, trying to see the game. After asking his driver to pull over, he got out of his car and said, 'Hey, what are you guys doing?'

"The four kids disentangled themselves from each other and ran away. They knew the man owned the team and feared they were in trouble.

"The next day the young fans could not stay away from the ballpark. But when they arrived at their viewing area, something was different.

"There were *four* holes in the fence—three of which were freshly drilled, each at a different elevation, each perfectly placed for the heights of the four fans.

"A message was painted above the holes. 'Enjoy the game!' is what it said. It was signed, 'Your Friend, the Owner.' And a note was taped to the fence. The tallest boy tore it open and read out loud. 'When we make the playoffs I'd like for you to watch the games with me—in my skybox.'"

"Wow!" Pete said as he scampered down from his father's arms. "Is that true? Did that really happen? Can we go see it?"

"Oh, even better than that, Pete," Jesna said with a smile.

"God has drilled four different holes for people to see his message through. They are the four Gospels. Each placed at a different vantage point—for ease of viewing. And he's definitely passing out skybox seats—for anyone who will take one."

"Wow!" Pete said. "Maybe that's why he began his book with 'In the big *inning* ...'"

When everybody had finished giggling, Priscilla asked another question. "Will you tell us about the four 'holes' in the fence? I'd like to know more about the Gospel writers."

"Yeah," Pete said. "I'd like to know which Gospel writer Zacchaeus liked best."

"Huh?" sang the Pilgrims.

"Well, he's about my height. I'm sure I'd like looking at Jesus through the same hole he does."

"I think you might have messed up another analogy, little brother," Priscilla said.

"Matthew," Jesna began, "was one of the twelve closest disciples of Jesus."

"And he was a tax grabber—before he got saved out of the world—huh, Jesna?"

"Yes, Pete, Matthew was a tax collector. His work was like that of an accountant today. It's probably not surprising that he began his Gospel by listing an orderly *account* of the genealogy of Jesus—divided into three neat sections with fourteen names in each.

"Matthew's interest in the 'bottom line' may have been behind the way he closed his record of Jesus' life. He ended it with the Great Commission scene.

"Matthew was sometimes called Levi. He was especially interested in Jewish readers and often reminded them of how the events of Jesus' life fulfilled Old Testament prophecies. He finished his Gospel just before A.D. 70.

"Mark, on the other hand," Jesna continued, "was more like a journalist. His is the most tightly written account. It's characterized by rapid action, vivid detail, and picturesque descriptions.

"Mark wasn't one of the original twelve disciples. He was a disciple of Peter. His Gospel is a written presentation of the teachings of Peter. Mark wrote his Gospel in Rome (before A.D. 70) and he, like Peter, had a special interest in the message getting out to the Gentiles.

"Like any good journalist, Mark got right to the point. He began his Gospel with a great lead sentence: 'The beginning of the gospel about Jesus Christ, the Son of God.'[94] No wasted words. And he gave God (his editor) two different places for ending the book (Mark 16:8 and Mark 16:20). The second ending reads like this:

> "And the disciples went everywhere preaching, the Master working right with them, validating the Message with indisputable evidence."[95]

"Now, Luke," Jesna continued, "was trained as a physician and historian. You can really see his historical side at the beginning of his Gospel. He says,

> "Therefore, since I myself have carefully investigated everything from the beginning, it seemed good also to me to write an orderly account for you...."[96]

"You can see his medical side coming through in his interest in miracles (especially the events surrounding Jesus' miraculous birth) and Jesus the Great Physician's 'prescriptions'—his parables on how to live.

"Luke was well educated in the Greek language and wrote with a Greek audience in mind. He was a Syrian from Antioch. While he was not one of the original twelve disciples either, he was one of the seventy whom Jesus sent out."

As Jesna finished telling us about Luke, we arrived back at our car. After we had taken a seat and strapped ourselves in, we blasted off. With colors aswirl, Jesna said, "I'll tell you about John when we land. We're going to his house right now."

FAMILY DISCUSSION

1. Now that you have "witnessed" all the scenes recorded in the four Gospels, what would your main emphasis be if you were going to write a book about the life of Jesus?
2. Share your idea with your family.

SCENE 236
THE ENDING OF JOHN[97]

"Everybody out for Asia Minor," Jesna announced like a miniature train conductor.

The world was standing still again. We had landed on a gently sloping hillside. It tumbled down in rolling waves of green to meet a huge body of water at a rocky border.

It appeared that we were all alone. But then my doggy nose told me otherwise. Over the wet smells of sea water, I picked up the unmistakable scent of a human.

There he was, about a hundred yards in front of us. A man was sitting in the shade of a leafy tree, amid a scattering of large rocks—about one good cat leap from the water's edge.

"Look over there, at the water's edge," Jesna instructed.

The Pilgrims began squinting. (Human eyes are so inferior, and don't even get me started about their pathetic noses.)

"Yeah," Pete was the first to announce. "I see him. Is he fishing?"

"No," Jesna said. "That's John. And he's putting the last words of his Gospel onto a scroll. John, you know, takes a whole different slant on Jesus' life—different, that is, from those of Matthew, Mark, and Luke.

"Hey," Jesna went on. "I'd love to know what each of you would emphasize if you were writing a Gospel. After all, you are eyewitnesses to the life of Jesus now."

"That's easy as pie!" Pete announced. "I'd tell everybody what a good friend Jesus was, to his disciples and to me, too. He just loved being with people. And he loved being alive in his Father's world.

"Oh yeah," Pete continued. "I'd tell about him calling God 'Daddy,' just like I do to my daddy. And he even said *we* could call God 'Daddy,' too. He said God *is* our Daddy. Wow! That's way cool, having Jesus as a best friend and God as your Daddy. Yep, that's what I'd write down."

Jesna was beaming. She must have thought Pete had gotten ahold of something really important.

"What about, you, Priscilla?" Jesna asked.

"Well," Priscilla said while staring up into her brain with her eyeballs. "I guess it was all the miracles that stood out to me. I mean, it's one thing to tell people they can start calling God their Father. But when the one who's saying that starts walking on water, telling the weather what to do, and raising people from the dead, well, that makes me pay close attention. After all, I know what the odds are for stuff like that to happen by chance."

"Me too," Pete interrupted. "It's zilch! And I don't even have a wrist computer to figure that out."

"You two are right," Jesna affirmed. "Jesus did more than

enough miracles to prove his right to make his claims."

"You know," Mr. Pilgrim began, ready now with *his* version of the Good News. "What made the biggest impression on me was how Jesus and the Pharisees kept butting heads. I mean, the Pharisees were the best keepers of the Law the world had ever seen, right? They were perfect in doing everything written down in Scripture. Yet they became Jesus' biggest critics—and he theirs."

"What do you make of that, Mr. Pilgrim?" Jesna asked.

"Maybe it's like when I took Pete to play Putt-Putt Golf."

"What?" Jesna asked.

"Well, Pete didn't know much about the game at the time. It was his first time out."

"But I picked it up real fast, huh, Dad?"

"'Fast' might be a little optimistic, Son. Because at first," Mr. Pilgrim continued, "you were just smacking that little ball against the bright orange planks. You'd hit it twenty or thirty times before it might 'accidentally' drop in the hole.

"And when it did, you seemed disappointed. But you'd pick up the ball and move on the next hole. Then you'd start putting dents in a new set of planks.

"It was all pretty funny for a while. But a big line started forming behind us. After a while I motioned them on through and took you over to the side."

"Hey, I remember this now, Dad. You showed me how to play, Dad. You stood behind me and showed me how to hold the club and swing it straight."

"Do you remember what else, Son?"

"Yeah, you told me to aim at the hole instead of the boards. And you bent over and showed me just how to do it, too."

"Yes," Mr. Pilgrim said. "And I believe that before we left, you got a hole-in-one."

"Yep, sure did."

"Well," Mr. Pilgrim continued. "That's why I think Jesus and the Pharisees butted heads so much."

"Huh?" everyone sang in a puzzled voice.

"The Pharisees were only focused on the planks. You know, the boundaries—the Law. And, unlike Pete, they weren't open to Jesus showing them how the game is supposed to be played. They just got mad at him for suggesting a new approach."

"Wow, Mr. Pilgrim!" Jesna said. "That's amazing. That's exactly what the problem was. And it explains why Jesus could say that he didn't come to change a jot or a tittle of the Law—while, at the same time, he changed everything."

"Jesus came to step *inside* his followers," Mr. Pilgrim said as his face grew animated. "He came to show us how to play the game of *life*. But if we refuse to let him, if we insist on playing our own way, he can't help us. It's our false sense of self-reliance that keeps us out of his kingdom."

"Yeah," Pete said. "And the people who aren't even playing between the planks are better off than the Pharisees. Even if they're smacking the ball around in the parking lot, they're better off. Because, if they'll just come up to Jesus and say, 'Mr. Jesus, will you please teach me how to play?' well, I bet he'll start smiling and step inside 'em. Then they'll be able to get a holiness-in-one—while those stubborn Pharisees are still bouncing off the planks."

A chorus of laughter erupted, followed by a sea of nodding heads.

Jesna seemed very satisfied. After a while she said, "What about you, Mrs. Pilgrim? We haven't heard what you would put in your Gospel."

"Oh," Mrs. Pilgrim began, "I'd have to say that Jesus' teaching about the kingdom is what stood out the most to me. I think it was the one thing he talked about every day. To me, his telling folks about the kingdom was the whole reason he put being God on hold and came to earth as a human being. He came to tell the world about his Father's kingdom. And he came to invite us all to live there, a little bit now, and a whole lot later."

Jesna was nodding a very satisfied head. "Mission accomplished," she whispered. And then, even more quietly, as she stared up into the heavens, "To you be the glory, Father."

After she let out a long, slow breath, Jesna opened her eyes wide and said, "Now, let's go see what John's up to."

We began to walk over to where John was sitting under a tree by the seaside. As we strolled, Jesna told us a bit about John's Gospel.

"You already know that Matthew, Mark, and Luke were primarily focused on communicating with three different groups of people—"

"Yeah," Priscilla interrupted. "And I just thought of something. Each of those groups—Jews, Gentiles, and Greeks—represented the three main languages spoken in Jerusalem: Hebrew, Latin, and Greek."

"Very good, Priscilla," Jesna said. "And that brings us to John. He was an expert in another language. John was able to understand the language of the heart. His Gospel is the *spiritual* Gospel. John was able to see things that can sail right past most folks."

"Like what?" Priscilla asked.

"Like the fact that God *spoke* the world into existence in the first book of the Bible. Then, at the start of the New Testament, He *speaks* redemption into existence—through the *Word,* his Son, Jesus.

"And, it's John who *sees* that people are like the pots at the wedding feast—earthen containers in need of being filled with a wholly new substance. It's John who *notices* we are *temples* of God's presence (houses of prayer)—temples in need of a good house cleaning.

"And it's John who underlines many other great visual parables—about new birth and baptism, sheep and goats, shepherds and the Good Shepherd. John's the one who emphasizes being in intimate relationship with the King—more so than the kingdom itself. It's he who says we should learn to know the Shepherd-King's voice.

"And speaking of intimacy, John devotes one third of his Gospel to one twenty-four-hour period—Jesus' last day with his friends. He makes sure we see the connection between the Lord's Supper and staying plugged into God—like branches into a vine. His Gospel focuses on intimate, spiritual relationship with God—our new-lesson-teaching, miracle-working Daddy."

Jesna's words brought us to the old apostle's side near the sea. John had just placed the stick he'd been writing with on a rock and allowed his head to rest against the tree trunk behind him.

I peered over his shoulder. The lines on the paper looked like the mess a chicken might make in the dirt with its feet. But Jesna was able to read to us the last words of John's Gospel.

"There are so many other things Jesus did. If they were all written down, each of them, one by one, I can't imagine a world big enough to hold such a library of books."[98]

"The End," Pete whispered.

FAMILY DISCUSSION

1. What does it mean to say that John saw Jesus through "spiritual eyes"?
2. Who is your favorite Gospel writer? Why?

SCENE 237
A FINAL WITNESS: PAUL'S ACCOUNT OF THE APPEARANCES OF JESUS[99]

"Let's allow John to rest," Jesna whispered. "He's earned it."

We all began to back away from the sleeping apostle. The completed Gospel was resting in his lap, the last words of which were being dried by the gentle sea breeze.

We climbed into the car. No sooner were our safety belts fastened than Jesna launched us straight up. We raced for the ceiling of the blue sky like a rocket. Within seconds the wispy white clouds that had been above were below, then way below.

When we completed our blast into the heavens we were looking down on the New Testament world—as astronauts would see it from the window of the space shuttle.

From our vantage point, Italy was a boot and Sicily a football. Spain looked like a lion's head and the Nile River a discarded string.

Jesna hit the buttons that sent us through time. But nothing swirled. "From way up here," she explained, "there isn't much change to see in just a few decades of time. But so you'll

know, we're going forward a few years."

She forgot to say we were also going down! After hitting the last button we began to fall like an elevator with snapped cables. I was swallowing hard and often to keep my stomach in place.

"See down there?" Jesna asked.

But everyone except Pete had their eyes sealed shut.

"That speck on the sea coast of what you call Turkey is the port city of Ephesus. The apostle Paul is there right now. He's writing a letter to the Christians in Corinth. I wanted you to see him—and something he's writing—before we go."

"I just want to see another tomorrow!" Mrs. Pilgrim shrieked.

"Oh, excuse me," Jesna said. And then she punched some buttons that caused us to slow to the more normal speed of a runaway train.

"Hey!" Pete said. "What's the deal? I was enjoying that."

Ephesus, our target, was growing in size. Judging from the number of stone-colored buildings and ships in its harbor, it was a center of commerce.

We leveled off and began to *swoosh* through the streets—about ten feet above dirt-and-cobblestone level. It wasn't long before Jesna took a sharp right—right through the walls of a modest rock house.

Mercifully, we came to a stop about ten feet from two men who were sharing a wooden table. One of them was talking. The other was scribbling with a stick.

"See?" Jesna said. "The man on the right is Paul."

"Wow!" Pete exclaimed. "He's the guy that wrote the rest of the New Testament."

"Well," Jesna said, "at least a good portion of it."

"Should I call him Saul or Paul?" Pete asked.

"Neither!" his mother shout-whispered.

"Why do you suppose God changed his name in the first place?" Pete continued.

"Because," Jesna said, "it helps to emphasize how different his life became after his conversion. You probably remember from Sunday school how 'Saul' was the son of a Pharisee. He was sent to Jerusalem at age thirteen to study under the famous Rabbi, Gamaliel. In fact he became such a devout defender of the faith that he was seen as a leader of those trying to destroy the followers of Christ.

"You remember, when Stephen was stoned to death," Jesna continued, "the rock-throwers put their coats at Saul's feet. Saul was an incredible mixture of the three main cultures of his day. He was a devout Jew, a Roman citizen, and a beneficiary of Greek culture and language. He was just what God was looking for to tell the world about the life, death, and resurrection of his Son, Jesus."

"Just one problem, though, huh, Jesna?"

"What's that, Pete?"

"Saul was killing Christians, not trying to make new ones."

"That's right, Pete. But God took care of that."

"Uh-humph," Pete said. "He blinded him with a blast of light and sent him off to Bible School in the desert."

"Yes, Pete. You're right. And now Christianity's most fervent destroyer has this to say in Christ's defense. Listen."

We stopped talking and trained our ears to the words 'Paul' was speaking to a human tape recorder—his scribe.

"The first thing I did was place before you what was placed emphatically before me: that the Messiah died for our sins, exactly as Scripture tells it; that he was buried; that he was raised from death on the third day, again exactly as Scripture says; that he presented himself alive to Peter, then to his closest followers, and later to more than five hundred of his followers all at the same time, most of them still around (although a few have since died); that he then spent time with James and the rest of those he commissioned to represent him; and that he finally presented himself alive to *me*. It was fitting that I bring up the rear. I don't deserve to be included in that inner circle, as you well know, having spent all those early years trying my best to stamp God's church right out of existence.

"But because God was so gracious, so very generous, here I am. And I'm not about to let his grace go to waste."[100]

"And," Jesna said to us, "that's exactly what God wants from each of you. You've seen his Son. Enjoy that grace. Don't let it go to waste."

"No way!" Pete said for us all. "I won't waste a drop."

FAMILY DISCUSSION

1. Reflect for a while on how powerful Paul's testimony must have been—a chief prosecutor of Christianity becoming a chief promoter.
2. Now consider how powerful Paul's testimony was that the Christ who was raised from the dead appeared to him personally.

SCENE 238
JESNA SAYS GOODBYE

"Everyone still buckled in?" Jesna asked.

"Yep," Pete answered for all.

With that Jesna began to program our car—for Daffy World, I guessed.

After punching a series of buttons, she reached into a compartment and handed out sunglasses. Yep, I was right about Daffy World. We wore sunglasses only for traveling across the centuries. Long-distance time travel always causes light to become very intense. Priscilla helped me put on my doggy pair of shades.

Then Jesna turned and punched the last button. It was a green one marked "Home."

Swoosh! We left Ephesus like a bullet in front of a gunpowder blast. We exploded through a quick flash of swirling colors and entered into the center of a bright beam of light. Yes, Pete's hands were over his head.

Then, after a time of being light, some unseen hand turned the flashlight off. It disappeared with a loud, fading hum. Our motion stopped.

We were back inside the giant dome we had left thirty-three Bible years ago. The ceiling was still out of sight. The floor was still as black and shiny as a waxed seal.

The mammoth room was dimly lit by wispy white lights that glowed faintly in the distance like electrified clouds.

To my right were the same two golden doors we had passed through back when we had begun the ride.

"Wow!" Pete exclaimed as he leapt from the car. "That was the best ride of my whole life. Can we go again? I ain't even hungry."

No one responded. Perhaps they were in shock. Or perhaps

they had already caught on to the sadness of the moment. We would soon be saying goodbye to Jesna.

"Jesna," Pete said, "how about coming home with us? You can go to school with me tomorrow and tell all my friends what you do for a living. And if you can take this car along … well, we'd be able to reinvent recess."

Jesna led the rest of us from the vehicle. She stood next to Pete and began studying his face—which was doing its part to light up the room. Her lips had formed a smile but her eyes weren't cooperating.

"I'm afraid I can't do that, Pete. As much as I'd like to. But I've got a secret to tell you. I'm not a tour guide like this all the time. I was on special assignment to be with you all."

"My goodness!" Pete exclaimed. "For an amateur, you sure know your stuff. You ought to consider this kinda work full-time. You're a natural!"

Jesna was blushing.

Pete continued on in rapid fire. I think he was afraid that if he stopped talking he'd start crying. "Then what is your full-time job, Jesna?"

"I'm an angel, Pete. I've been a full-time angel for a long time."

"Wow! I've never met an angel before. You mean you've been one since back before the Internet?"

"Further back."

"Before there was baseball or bubble gum or cars?"

"No, I mean way, way back. Since before there were things like earth, planets, or comets. Since before the great rebellion."

"No wonder you're the smartest kid I've ever met!"

That brought a giggle to Jesna's face. It had been trying to show two emotions at once. "I'm really going to miss you,

Pete." Then looking into everyone's faces, she said, "I'm going to miss each of you, very, very much."

Jesna's face had made up its mind. It became a wellspring for tears. At that everyone's eyes turned into salty fountains.

Pete put a bear hug around Jesna's neck. Priscilla threw her arms around her from the other side. Mr. and Mrs. Pilgrim hit their knees and formed an outer ring. I stood on my hind legs and got a paw in myself.

Always the perfect guide, Jesna allowed herself to be the centerpiece of the vertical dog pile for a long time. Then, after we'd put out enough water to drown a forest fire, Jesna whispered, "It's time for me to go now."

We all disentangled, like depressed zombies.

"I'll miss you," Mr. Pilgrim sobbed.

"We all will," echoed Mrs. Pilgrim.

"Yeah," Priscilla began. "I don't know if I'll still be able to think with my heart without you around."

"And I might not be able to think with my head," Pete added. "My stomach might take over again."

"You will all do just great," Jesna said. "And besides, that's one of the best things about being part of the kingdom. You never have to say a final goodbye. Never. Just, 'See you later.'"

"We say, 'Smell ya later,'" Pete offered, giving me a knowing look and patting my head.

But I'm not sure Jesna heard that. She had already begun to fade into thin air. Before she was completely invisible, though, she kissed the palm of her hand and tossed it to us.

We all participated in a long and loud sigh. Then we turned and walked toward the golden doors.

"I bet that Jesna is the coolest angel in heaven," Pete sighed.

"You said it, little brother," Priscilla agreed. And then she draped an arm around Pete's neck and pulled him close. "She helped me find my heart *and* my little brother."

FAMILY DISCUSSION

1. Is there anything you found while being on the Bible Ride?

SCENE 239
FIRST ATTEMPTS AT TELLING THE WORLD

As we approached the gigantic golden gate that separated our ride from the amusement park's lesser attractions, it began to slide inward. The doors moved automatically and without a sound.

We passed through and found ourselves back at the maze of rails that led to the set of rusty metal doors. As we walked through the labyrinth in single file, Priscilla's watch beeped.

"Wow!" she said. "It's 1:31:00, just like Jesna said. I set my watch to see if we'd really make it back in less than sixty seconds. I thought it would beep before the ride ever left! Thirty-three Bible years ago!"

"That wasn't the only thing Jesna was right about," Mrs. Pilgrim said to her husband while inspecting the location of Priscilla's arm. It was still encircling Pete's neck. And he wasn't complaining! "She said sixty seconds would be enough time for your whole world to be turned 'upside down and inside out.'"

"Hmm," Priscilla went on, unaware of her mother's comments, her eyes still glued to the face of her watch. "Time must start playing at a different speed as soon as you're on the other side of those golden doors. 'Cause we were saying good-bye to Jesna for more than a minute."

"I guess some things do stay the same, though," Mr. Pilgrim said with a wink at his wife and a nod in the direction of the two youngest Pilgrims. "Wouldn't you say so, Honey?"

Pete had begun to dig in the deepest depths of his pockets—for anything edible, I would assume. With her arm still around Pete's neck, Priscilla was punching at her watch while trying to avoid choking her little brother.

We arrived at the rusty metal doors. They had to be pushed open manually. Mr. Pilgrim did the honors. As the right door gave way to his assault and inched its way outward, a flood of light poured into the room.

"Humph," Pete said. "Traveling around thought-time with an angel makes plain ole earth-light seem pretty dull—like my night light next to a bonfire. I hope I can get used to it."

We then navigated the final maze of rails. I was beginning to feel a little like a lab rat. At the end of the metalwork was the cross-shaped opening in a wooden fence. We squeezed through it—the entrance and exit to the Bible Ride.

Back in the other world, things hadn't changed much in sixty seconds. The park was still overflowing with odd-shaped humans, each trying to be amused. The smells of the four basic food groups—frying fat, sugar, ice cream, and soda—were thick in the air.

"Look!" Pete exclaimed. "There he is. That same big ole man with the hairy back. The one we were behind when we were in line for the Dragon Master. Do you think he remembers us after all these Bible years? Maybe he'd let us back in line. Hey, let's go get us some five-gallon cherry slushies and ask him if he'll let us cut."

"Yes, I see your point," Mrs. Pilgrim whispered to her husband. "Some things are impervious to change."

But no sooner were the words out of her mouth than Pete surprised us all.

"No, I've got a better idea," he said. "Let's go and tell everybody they need to go on the Bible Ride. Let's tell 'em what we know—that it's the best ride in the whole park. Let's tell 'em that if they want to meet a *real* Dragon Master, they need to see how Jesus does it. After all, that's what we promised him we'd do."

"Son," Mr. Pilgrim said, "I think that's the best idea that ever found its way out of your mouth. Let's do it!"

And with that each was off in a different direction—north, south, east, and west. But no one had to travel more than a few yards before finding someone—of similar height—to tell about the Bible Ride. I stayed behind and barked my support as the Pilgrims started ride-hawking with more energy than a carnival owner. If another dog had been around, I would've been doing the same.

I think Jesna, and especially Jesus, would've been proud of the four Pilgrim apostles. What am I saying? I think they both *are* proud.

But then something strange began to happen. And then, something even stranger.

No one listened to the four Pilgrims for very long. Human after human walked away from them. Some were laughing. Some looked frightened. Some pulled their arms back with a jerk, and others snapped out angry words.

I wondered if the people were frightened by the Pilgrims' excitement. I wondered if they didn't believe them.

But I didn't have much time to speculate. Because at that moment I saw Pete grab hold of a man's shirt. It was the father of a boy he'd been unable to convince.

When Pete had the man's full attention, he turned and

began pointing at the ride. But then Pete's jaws dropped open. His eyes became as wide as saucers and he turned ghost white. His hand fell from the man's shirt.

"Hey!" he exclaimed. "Mom! Dad! Where's the Bible Ride!!??"

I turned around. It was gone. Nothing stood where it had been except a grove of trees. I took two steps back and started howling like a mad dog.

SCENE 240

THE CONCLUSION, AND THE BEGINNING

When I came to my doggy senses, I looked over at the Pilgrims. They were huddled together in a fort of mutual comfort. If they felt like I did, kudzu vines of tangled emotions were growing in their stomachs.

I leapt over to where they were standing and entered the bulwark their group hug had made.

Pete was the first to speak. He was ghostly white.

"Dad, Mom, we *did* spend the last thirty-three years together, didn't we?"

"Y-yes, Son," Mrs. Pilgrim said in an unsure voice. "I'm sure we did … I think."

"This is like that *Twilight Zone* show on TV," Priscilla said. "I'm staring at five trees in an empty lot. But I know I got on a ride there. I know I walked where Jesus walked. I walked *with* him! But did I dream it? Did I just doze off?"

"Well, Prissy," Mr. Pilgrim began, "if you dreamed it, we all had the exact same dream. But I'll say this. The most incredible thing I've ever experienced in my life just got multiplied times a hundred."

"Times a million, Dad," Pete said. "'Cause look at this!"

Pete had retrieved something from his pocket. He held it out for us all to see.

"Pete!" exclaimed Mrs. Pilgrim. "You shouldn't have taken that! But ... I'm sure glad you did!"

In the center of Pete's glistening palm rested a silver coin. A denarius. Caesar's face was shiny and new.

"You'd better put that in a safe place, Son," Mr. Pilgrim said. "We may need to show it to someone—to stay out of the loony bin."

Mr. Pilgrim had spoken as a prophet. No sooner had those words crossed his teeth than a team of blue-uniformed men approached. Only one of them was packing a gun, but each was wearing a badge pinned to his uniform. That is, all but one. He was wearing a black suit and tie. He seemed to be in charge. He was the first to speak.

"Is there something I can help you folks with?"

"No," Mr. Pilgrim croaked. "We're just fine."

"Well," the black-suited man continued, "some of our guests have said that you may be experiencing some difficulties."

"I'll say we are!" Pete began. "We got on one of your rides over there and got whisked off through the pages of the Bible! We had a little ole angel for a tour guide—man, she was smart—and we were with Jesus, every day, for about thirty-three years...."

Flop! Mr. Pilgrim put his hand over Pete's mouth. "Uh, that is, what he meant to say is, uh, we've really enjoyed being at Daffy World. It's been great."

"So," the man in black began, "what your son said isn't true? He's a little confused?"

"Well," said Mr. Pilgrim, "I wouldn't exactly say that."

"Dad? Aren't you going to tell him what happened to us? Aren't you going to witness to everybody—like Jesus told us to do?"

"But, Son," Mr. Pilgrim whispered through clenched teeth. "I don't think they'll understand."

"I know, Dad. That's the same problem Jesus had. But you have to tell 'em anyway and leave the understanding in God's hands."

"But, Son …"

"So," the man in black said, "did you *all* see Jesus here at Daffy World or just the boy?"

"No!" Pete exclaimed.

"Well, that's a relief!" the man replied.

"We saw him in Jerusalem. And in Galilee. And places like that."

The color in the man's face drained into his collar.

"Did all of you see Jesus!?" he demanded. "Yes or no!"

"Yes," Mr. Pilgrim said. "But you need to hear the whole story."

"No! I don't! I can't have you frightening our guests with your wild, psychotic tales. You'll have to leave the park."

"Oh, that'll be fine," Mr. Pilgrim said.

"Sure," Pete volunteered. "We got more than our money's worth today. But you ought to take that ride yourself, Mister. Jesus could help you with that mean streak you got. (I used to have one, too.) You should've seen what he did to a man with a whole army of demons in him. Man, he made them things jump into some pigs, and—"

"Guards!" the man in black yelled. "Will you please show

this family the way to the exit? I'll radio ahead. There'll be a car waiting for them."

"Oh, that's OK," Mr. Pilgrim said. "We know the way out. And I even remember where we parked. 'D-7.' So we can see ourselves out."

But that wasn't good enough for the man in charge. He told us that his security guards would see us to the exit. And he said that we'd have to get in a special car when we got there. He was very insistent.

We were marched through the park like a flock of sheep—kept in line by a pack of sheep dogs. We walked in silence, and in shame. I don't remember feeling more confused in my whole doggy life. The Pilgrims seemed to feel worse than I did.

When we finally arrived at the front gate, a big white truck was there to meet us. It looked more like an ambulance than a car. "Bellevue Sanitorium" was painted on its side.

"Hey!" Mr. Pilgrim shouted. "What is this? We aren't getting in that thing. I know where you want to take us. You think we're nuts!"

"There ain't no thinking to it," one of the guards said. "And you *are* getting in. It's for your own good. Now, move it!"

The uniformed men had formed a human cattle ramp leading to the open doors of the white paddy wagon. There was nowhere to go but in.

The Pilgrims climbed into the vehicle. I leapt. We sat down on one of two rows of seats facing each other. No one else was in the back but us. The doors were slammed with a thud. It sounded like a jail door being shut … or like an explosion.

Immediately we pulled away from the curb. As the blue uniforms began to shrink in the glass panels of the rear doors, another white truck—exactly like ours—pulled up to the curb.

From a distance of about one hundred yards I could see that the guards began to wave their arms in the air and jump up and down. I think they were trying to get the attention of our driver.

I looked into the cab area. I couldn't see who was driving. Whoever it was was real short. I could only see the driver's eyes—in the rearview mirror. They looked really familiar.

Then the driver reached down and picked up a microphone to speak to us.

"Next stop," the driver said, "Eden. Better put your glasses on."

"Jesna!" four Pilgrims exclaimed.

But then the afternoon disappeared into a swirl of color. We were headed for a ride through the Old Testament. I just knew it!

ENDNOTES

Scene . . . . . Note

181 . . . . 1. From Matthew 26:1-5; Mark 14:1-2; Luke 22:1-2; John 11:47-53.

2. John 11:49b-50.

182. . . . . 3. From Matthew 26:14-16; Mark 14:10-11; Luke 22:3-6; John 13:2; 27, 6:70-71.

183. . . . . 4. From Matthew 26:17-20; Mark 14:12-17; Luke 22:7-14; John 13:1.

184. . . . . 5. From Matthew 23:6-12, 10:24, 40; Luke 22:3, 12:37, 22:24-28, 6:40, 10:16; John 13:1-20.

6. See Edersheim's *The Life and Times of Jesus the Messiah,* Book II, chapter 9.

7. John 13:12-17.

185. . . . . 8. From Matthew 26:21-25; Mark 14:18-21; Luke 22:21-23; John 13:21-30.

9. Matthew 26:23-24.

186. . . . . 10. From Matthew 26:26-29; Mark 14:22-25; Luke 22:15-20; John 6:51-58.

11. Matthew 26:27-29.

187. . . . . 12. From John 13:31-35.

13. John 13:33-35.

188. . . . . 14. From Matthew 26:30-35; Mark 14:26-31; Luke 22:31-34; John 13:36-38.

15. Matthew 26:31-32.

189. . . . . 16. From Luke 22:35-38.

17. Luke 22:38b.

190. . . . . 18. From John 14:1-14.

19. John 14:6-7.

20. John 14:11-14.

191. . . . . 21. From John 14:15-26.

22. John 14:15-17.

23. John 14:18-21.

24. John 14:25-26.

192. . . . . 25. From John 14:27-31.

26. John 14:27-31.

193. . . . . . . 27. From John 15:1-8.
28. John 15:5-8.
194 . . . . . . 29. From John 15:9-17.
30. John 15:9-17.
195 . . . . . . 31. From John 15:18-25.
32. John 15:18-25.
196. . . . . . . 33. From John 15:26-27.
34. John 15:26-27.
197. . . . . . . 35. From John 16:1-4.
36. John 16:1-4.
198. . . . . . . 37. From John 16:5-16.
38. John 16:5-16.
199 . . . . . . 39. From John 16:17-22.
40. John 16:19-22.
200. . . . . . . 41. From John 16:23-28.
42. John 16:23-28.
201 . . . . . . 43. From John 16:29-33.
44. John 16:31-33.
202 . . . . . . 45. From John 17:1-13.
46. John 17:1-13.
203. . . . . . . 47. From John 17:14-26.
48. John 17:14-26.
204 . . . . . . 49. From Matthew 26:36-46; Mark 14:32-42; Luke 22:39-46; John 18:1.
50. Matthew 26:38.
51. Matthew 26:39.
52. Matthew 26:40-42.
205. . . . . . . 53. From Matthew 26:47-56; Mark 14:43-52; Luke 22:47-53; John 18:2-11.
54. Matthew 26:52-54.
55. Matthew 26: 55-56.
206. . . . . . . 56. From Matthew 26:57-68; Mark 14:53-65; Luke 22:54-71; John 18:13-24.
207. . . . . . . 57. From Matthew 26:69-75; Mark 14:66-72; Luke 22:56-62; John 18:25-27.
208. . . . . . . 58. From Matthew 27:1-2; Mark 15:1; Luke 23:1; John 18:28.
209. . . . . . . 59. From Matthew 27:3-10.
210. . . . . . . 60. From Matthew 27:11-14; Mark 15:2-5; Luke 23:2-5; John 18:29-38.

211.......61. From Matthew 27:12; Mark 15:3-4; Luke 23:6-12.
212.......62. From Luke 23:13-16; John 18:38b.
63. Luke 23:14-16.
213.......64. From Matthew 27:15-23; Mark 15:6-14; Luke 23:17-23; John 18:39-40.
214.......65. From Matthew 27:27-31a; Mark 15:16-20a; John 19:2-3.
215.......66. From Matthew 27:31b-32; Mark 15:20b-21; Luke 23:26-32; John 19:17a.
67. Luke 23:28-31.
216.......68. From Matthew 27:33-37; Mark 15:22-26; Luke 23:33-34; John 19:18-24.
217.......69. From Matthew 27:38-43; Mark 15:27-32a; Luke 23:35-38; John 19:19-22.
218 ...... 70. From Matthew 27:44; Mark 15:32b; Luke 23:39-43.
219.......71. From Matthew 27:45-54; Mark 15:33-39; Luke 23:44-48; John 19:28-30.
220.......72. From Matthew 27:55-56; Mark 15:40-41; Luke 23:49; John 19:25-27.
221 ...... 73. From John 19:31-37.
222.......74. From Matthew 27:57-61; Mark 15:42-47; Luke 23:50-56; John 19:38-42.
223.......75. From Matthew 27:62-66.
224.......76. From Matthew 28:1-8; Mark 16:1-8; Luke 24:1-12; John 20:1-13.
225.......77. From Matthew 28:9-10; Mark 16:9-11; Luke 24:10-11; John 20:14-18.
226.......78. From Matthew 28:11-15.
227.......79. From Mark 16:12-13; Luke 24:13-35
80. Luke 24:19b-24.
228.......81. From Luke 24:36-43; John 20:19-23
229.......82. From John 20:24-29.
83. Hebrews 11:1.
230.......84. From Mark 16:14-18.
85. Mark 16:15-16.
231 ...... 86. From Luke 5:1-11; John 21:1-14.
232.......87. From John 21:15-19.
233.......88. From Matthew 28:16-20.
89. Matthew 28:18-20.
234.......90. From Mark 16:15, 19; Luke 24:44-53.

91. Luke 24:44.
92. Luke 24:46-47a.
235.......93. From Mark 16:19-20.
94. Mark 1:1, NIV.
95. Mark 16:20.
96. Luke 1:3a, NIV.
236.......97. From John 21:24-25.
98. John 21:24-25.
237.......99. From 1 Corinthians 15:3-12.
100. 1 Corinthians 15:3-12.